FRIENDS

LIKE

THESE

FRIENDS

LIKE

THESE

MEG

ROSOFF

BLOOMSBURY

LONDON OXFORD NEW YORK NEW DELHI SYDNEY

BLOOMSBURY YA
Bloomsbury Publishing Plc
50 Bedford Square, London WC1B 3DP, UK
29 Earlsfort Terrace, Dublin 2, Ireland

BLOOMSBURY, BLOOMSBURY YA and the
Diana logo are trademarks of Bloomsbury Publishing Plc

First published in Great Britain in 2022 by Bloomsbury Publishing Plc

A catalogue record for this book is available from the British Library

ISBN: HB: 978-1-5266-4611-8; TPB: 978-1-5266-4613-2;
eBook: 978-1-5266-4608-8

2 4 6 8 10 9 7 5 3 1

Typeset by RefineCatch Limited, Bungay, Suffolk

Printed and bound in Great Britain by CPI Group (UK) Ltd, Croydon CR0 4YY

To find out more about our authors and books visit www.bloomsbury.com
and sign up for our newsletters

For Paul. Ever and always

1

Arriving in New York for the first time was like wearing a sign that said CHEAT ME.

Muggers mugged. Junkies jacked up. Pickpockets picked pockets. Flashers flashed, rapists raped and perverts perved. Psycho bag ladies shouted obscenities at miscellaneous crazies. You could get shot just for being in the path of a bullet. AIDS knew where you lived.

Heaps of garbage stank on every corner. Taxis honked, hawkers shouted, brakes screamed. Women jeered, flirted, complained in a barely comprehensible language. *Gedda hell oudda heah! Don' fuckwidme mistah*. The midday sun bounced off ten million glaring surfaces.

Dragging her suitcase out of the station on the hottest day of the year, Beth dripped sweat. Signs made unhelpful suggestions: Seventh Avenue, Eighth. Thirty-first Street. Thirty-third. She didn't dare ask directions for fear of being taken for a fool. Or worse, a tourist.

She stuck out her arm and a taxi swerved. Shoving her suitcase on to the seat, she fell in after it and closed the door.

'Christopher Street,' she gasped, hoping he'd know where that was. And then, just like that, they were off. The sweet smell of decay blew in through the open window mixed with exhaust fumes and melted tar.

Beth sat back in the cab and sighed. *Remember this time and place*, she thought. *New York City, June 1983. This is where it starts.*

Already her life felt like a miracle.

2

'Which corner?' In the mirror the driver waited for an answer, rolled his eyes.

Which corner? She frowned. Why did it matter?

He screeched to a halt. 'Two thirty-five,' he said, shaking his head, thinking (no doubt) he could have charged this girl anything.

She fumbled in her purse, found three dollars, handed it over, threw open the door and fell out on to the melting sidewalk with her bag.

'Keep the change,' she whispered as he sped away.

The lock on the building's front door was broken. Inside, a single bulb illuminated peeling paint and a row of dented metal mailboxes. The heat was unbearable. She hauled her suitcase to the foot of the stairs and began to climb, stopping on each landing to wipe the sweat from her hands.

On the fifth floor she flicked the light switch and recoiled.

A figure sat slumped against the door, glaring. 'It's about fucking time. I've been waiting in this hell-hole all day.'

Beth gaped.

'Open the door, for fuck's sake.' The strange girl snatched Beth's keys. 'I'll do it,' she said, pushing her own suitcase in first. 'Christ what a fucking dump.'

'I'm …'

'I know who you are. You're Rachel's friend. Bernie. Betsy. Barbie.'

'Beth.'

A dark hall led to a tiny living room (no window) with a door on each side. The kitchen was only big enough for one person, the bathroom too small for a sink. A definite scurrying in her peripheral vision when she turned on the light. Cockroaches.

The apartment came furnished. In the living room, a Chinese scroll hung sideways over a small oatmeal-coloured sofa, like you'd find in a dentist's waiting room. A wooden folding chair and a small glass coffee table completed the suite. The only shelf held a dusty wine bottle covered in drips.

Rachel's sister dumped her bag in the near bedroom and ran the water in the kitchen, waiting unsuccessfully for it to cool. 'I'm Dawn. Tom should be here already. He has the keys.'

Beth hated people referring to strangers as if you should know them. Who was Tom? Her boyfriend? Her cat?

'Oh,' Beth said. 'Thanks for letting me live here.'

'Couldn't afford it without you. Have to find a job. You got one, right?' She looked Beth up and down, as if to say, *If you got a job, I can get ten.*

Beth nodded.

'We've got to do something about this place. I can't live in a fucking slum.'

'Do you mind if …' Beth edged towards the door.

'Be my guest.'

Beth dragged her bag into the second bedroom. Small double bed, narrow bedside table, chest of drawers. Barely room for a person. Bare bulb overhead.

How could it be so hot?

Across the way, a brick tenement identical to theirs had fire escapes running up and down like zips on a biker jacket. She opened the window and stuck her head out over the street, desperate for air. A muffled clamour rose from below. It was hotter outside than in.

Stripping off her clothes, she fell back on the bare mattress.

Ugh, she thought. *I need a shower.*

The door to Dawn's room was closed when Beth stepped out in a towel. She hurried to the bathroom, stood under the cold shower till her blood cooled, then stood dripping on the wet tile floor. No bath mat, no shower curtain. Water trickled from the ceiling and ran down the walls; the entire apartment had become a rainforest. She was sweating again by the time she reached her bedroom.

Beth made the bed and unpacked into the chest of drawers. A few stray items at the back – green nylon underpants, torn T-shirt, single grey sock – she dumped guiltlessly in the trash.

And that was it. Home.

Lying naked on the bed, she spread the damp towel over her torso. If you didn't move, it wasn't too bad.

As the light slipped away, Beth heard a male voice in the next room. *Must be Tom*, she thought. Not a cat then. She lacked the energy to check. It was too hot to get dressed. Too hot to talk. Definitely too hot to talk to Dawn.

Outside, singing, swearing and shouting rose up in a spew of noise. New York City after dark sounded savage.

She turned off the light and tried to sleep.

3

The next morning, Beth woke early, dressed and went out. The bars on Christopher Street were closed, clientele gone to their beds or someone else's. Ten minutes of wandering led her to The Acropolis, a blue, white and chrome Greek coffee shop. Within seconds she'd been steered to a counter seat, a menu slapped in front of her.

'Coffee?' The waiter held up a pot.

She nodded, grateful. He filled a heavy white mug and slid a metal container of milk in front of her.

Beth ordered the Breakfast Special – two eggs any style, pancakes, hash browns, bacon, sausage and toast. She hadn't eaten since breakfast the day before. Her plate arrived with far too much food, but she ate it all, accepting extra toast and coffee because it was free. The waiters treated her with reassuring indifference.

After breakfast, with no desire to encounter Dawn and Tom, she set off exploring. From the air-conditioned coffee shop, outdoors hit her like a hammer. Not even ten and already creeping up towards a hundred degrees.

She walked and walked. And looked and looked. And walked. And looked. Veered into a pizza joint.

'Please,' she said. 'Could I please have some water ...'

The pizza man filled a giant waxed cup with water and ice. He waved when she reached for her wallet. 'I'm not gonna charge you for ice.'

Her hands, thick with heat, dipped into the cup.

For hours, Beth sat in Washington Square watching people come and go. All around her, New

Yorkers in sunglasses, stiletto heels, flip-flops and roller skates flowed from here to there and back again, impervious to weather and everything else.

Eventually she got up and wandered off again through the streets. She stopped at a store advertising air-con and exotic gifts, with hash pipes, ropes of silver jewellery, T-shirts printed with marijuana leaves and books of Indian poetry in the window. Inside it stank of patchouli. She took her time, searching the glass cases as if for something specific, though the salesgirl ignored her. Wreathed in cool air, Beth's eyes glazed over with pleasure. Could she stay here all day?

Her damp clothes began to turn icy.

'You need help?' The girl looked up at last. She was young, hippieish.

Beth pointed to a large black-and-white poster of Debbie Harry looking sideways at the camera. 'How much is that?'

'It's the last one and it's torn. You can have it for a

buck.' Not waiting for assent, the girl pulled it off the wall and rolled it up.

'You want the tacks?'

Beth nodded and exchanged them for a damp dollar bill from her pocket. Indian goat bells tinkled on the door as she left.

For a few seconds the heat outside was bliss.

Box fans formed a pyramid in front of a hardware store. *Get 'Em While They're Hot* said the handwritten sign. She bought one, and a cheap desk lamp.

Back on her block, the party she'd heard the night before was in full swing. It wasn't frightening down here, just giddy and feverish. Men in tight satin micro shorts or jeans and tank tops arrived outside bars where people already gathered to drink, talk, hold hands and kiss. Couples dressed head to toe in leather strolled past oblivious to the heat. She'd never noticed gay people back home; they all must live here.

Beth threw her shoulder at the front door and

flicked on the light. The bulb blew with a flash and she trudged up to 5E in the dark.

Nobody home, much to her relief. Dumping her treasures on the bed, she set up her new lamp. It was better than the ghoulish overhead but nothing could fix the depressing atmosphere of the place. The only cheering feature was a slim bookcase pushed up against the living-room wall, with best-sellers from past years, a few classics, and half a dozen old books with brightly illustrated covers. Some previous tenant had been a reader. She plugged in the fan and switched it to high, then stood on her bed to hang the poster. Tacks slid easily into the flimsy wall.

Beth stepped back. Debbie Harry looked strong. *I will surround myself with strong women*, she thought. *And become like them.*

Stripping down to her T-shirt, she dozed off to the noisy whoosh of the fan, waking early evening in a drugged haze, her sheets damp with sweat, hungry but unwilling to brave the endless stairs. From the corner of her eye she glimpsed scuttling.

Both windows faced the street so there was no chance of a cross-breeze. Beth soaked her T-shirt in cold water and wore it to bed. When she woke at midnight it was bone-dry, so she soaked it once more and went back to sleep, clammy, hot and cold at once.

From deep within a heat-haze dream she heard Dawn and Tom come in.

Saturday night on Christopher Street sounded like an insurrection.

4

For her interview six months earlier, Beth told the story of her best friend's rejection from the local high school, despite living practically next door. Innocent questions turned serious when she uncovered exclusions that didn't chime with local zoning. Why were some students admitted and some not, given equal proximity?

She went to town council meetings and asked school board members questions about quotas and pupil places. No one thought to lie to a seventeen-year-old. What she found revealed admission practices based on religion and race, and when the school newspaper chose not to run the story, Beth took it to the local news. National wires picked it up and within days it was headlining in New York, Washington, DC and Chicago.

'HIGH SCHOOL SLEUTH BUSTS ZONING CHEATS' and 'SHOCK SCHOOL QUOTA COVER-UP'. The headlines made her temporarily famous and guaranteed the internship against steep competition.

The answer came first by letter, then by phone.

'Hello, Beth?'

'Yes?'

'It's Jeanne Pearce in New York. I just wanted to congratulate you in person. We were very impressed by your application.'

'Thank you.' She felt a surge of triumph.

'The summer term runs from June twentieth to Labor Day. Will you have trouble finding a place to stay in New York?'

'No, it's OK. My friend's sister has a sublet.'

'Excellent. That's Monday the twentieth at nine.

Your first test is to find us.' She chuckled. 'Unless you have questions, I'll see you then.'

On Sunday, Beth returned to The Acropolis where the waiter confirmed her table for one and tossed down a menu. But then he turned round and said, 'Breakfast Special over easy? Coffee extra toast?'

It was like receiving a key to the city.

Afterwards she practised walking to work. Forty blocks, forty minutes, straight up Seventh Avenue in the sweltering heat, through the plant district, the garment district; past groups of men hanging around outside Spanish bodegas and Cuban Chinese diners, smoking, reading newspapers, arguing. The only immediate danger was heatstroke. Despite every-thing she'd heard about New York, none of it seemed particularly threatening.

At Times Square, she walked slowly past the bronze revolving doors, then turned and retraced her steps back down Seventh Avenue, not yet confident enough to try a different route.

Halfway to the Village she passed a store with neon T-shirts in the window and, inside, a gigantic industrial fan, big as an airplane engine. Beth went in and stood in the powerful breeze like a seagull coasting an updraught. It was no weather to be trying on clothes. The salesgirl, languid and slow, approached with an armful of hangers.

'Try this,' she said, holding out a loose cotton jumpsuit. It was tobacco brown, sleeveless with a deep V-neck. 'Leave your T-shirt on.'

Beth held her arms away from her sides and stepped into the jumpsuit. The salesgirl chose a wide leather belt, fastened it around her waist and looked at her dispassionately.

The jumpsuit looked great but the person in the mirror was wrong. Wrong hair, wrong shoes, wrong way of standing. The expression on her face was wrong. Her parents, home-town, school, friends, aspirations. All wrong.

'See?' said the girl.

She saw.

Beth bought the jumpsuit and belt, plus a black-and-white-striped skirt her mother would hate and a tight neon pink T-shirt. Elation competed with despair. How could her life possibly live up to her new clothes? Three crumbs of fashion was more a curse than a fix, throwing the horror of her existing wardrobe into stark relief. Well, at least she'd have something to wear on the first day.

She left the shop. Her feet hurt. Her sneakers smelled bad. She'd spent most of her money. Vendors called out to her: 'Louis Vuitton bags! Cartier watches! Top quality Ray-Bans! Get yer Gucci loafers, Versace jeans, Lacoste sun hats! Wind-up toys, books, belts, jewellery!' Wherever she looked, gigantic boom boxes howled dance music from people's shoulders.

No one had ever been more grateful for New York's special gift to newcomers: anonymity.

She bent to examine the Rolex watches, twenty

dollars each, two for thirty. Gigantic, tacky, flashy things. They looked real enough to her. How could you tell?

The air of New York was thick with repartee. Women argued prices with street hawkers, beggars mumbled if you flipped them a quarter, roller skaters bantered their way backwards along crowded sidewalks. One guy smelling of urine held a sign that read *Raising $10 million for wine research*. Beth's head swam with the noise.

As the day wore on, her skin turned grey with dust. There didn't seem to be enough air in the air. *It might make sense to eat dinner now*, she thought, though it was only four thirty. No way would she risk opening the apartment's fridge. Anything could be in there. A cockroach colony. A severed head. She bought an ice-cream cone, licking the drips as fast as they melted, and suddenly realised how tired she was. Back on Christopher Street, she opened the lobby door and began the long trudge to the fifth floor.

Dawn was home, eating cheesy Goldfish out of the bag and drinking beer. 'What you got there? You been shopping?'

'A few things for work tomorrow. Jesus it's hot in here. I got a fan yesterday – you should get one. There's a hardware place a block over selling them.'

'Supposed to be like this all summer. Fucking awful if it is. No way I'm going up and down those fucking stairs ever again. Tom will do it.'

Beth wondered if Dawn planned to spend the entire summer in the apartment. She wondered if she'd ever meet Tom. Maybe he was just a voice.

She retreated, turned the fan on high and closed her door. The breeze swept the corners of the room in ragged circles like a trapped pigeon.

5

Arriving at work on Monday morning dressed for the Sahara, Beth found the temperature inside arctic. Everyone else, she noticed, carried a sweater or jacket.

In the lobby, Jeanne introduced them – Oliver, Dan, Beth and Edie.

The other three turned to look at Beth. Anyone aspiring to be a journalist knew about her big story.

The male interns stood together – tall Oliver in horn-rimmed glasses and a sand-coloured suit, and Dan, keen as a Dobermann, practically dancing on the balls of his feet. Beth glanced twice at Oliver, almost handsome, with the long straight nose and ironical bearing of a nineteenth-century English-man. Dan looked faintly rock and roll in a narrow leather tie. Edie, standing apart, wore a neon orange minidress and green plastic earrings. She had short, bleached hair. Beth felt dull as a carp.

Oliver noticed her noticing.

Jeanne led them through to the cafeteria, ordered coffee and explained that Oliver and Dan would start in editorial and Edie and Beth in features, that they'd swap departments and partners as time went on. The other interns could obviously taste their Pulitzers for investigative reporting or, at the very least, droll restaurant and film reviews. Beth was happy just to be there.

'Remember, please,' Jeanne said with stern emphasis, as if reading their thoughts, 'that you are not cub reporters. The point of the internship is to experience everything and leave with an overview.'

Each was assigned an open cubicle opposite Jeanne's office.

While still reading over her agreement from personnel, Beth heard a *pssst* from above. Edie was standing on her desk, leaning over the top of the partition.

'Hey!' she said. 'You're the one who broke that high school scandal story, aren't you?'

Beth nodded.

'Wow. You busy for lunch?'

'No.'

'Good.' Edie disappeared.

At twelve thirty precisely, she reappeared at ground level and whispered, 'Come on,' loud enough to alert the boys. Beth, still struggling with her contract, jumped.

'Don't bother with that,' Edie said. 'You're not supposed to read it. Most of it's not true anyway. That stuff about evaluations and warnings? Forget it. They like you, you stay. They don't like you, your body gets washed up in the East River forty-eight hours later.'

Beth stared.

'And eaten by rats.'

'Actual rats?'

Edie nodded.

Beth thought for a moment. 'I don't like rats.'

'Nobody likes rats,' Edie said. 'Sandwich?'

'OK.'

'Let's go to the cafeteria. Then some place to warm up.'

Beth glanced sideways, lowered her voice. 'Should we ask the boys?'

Edie's answer was to open her eyes wide with mock horror. She headed out and Beth followed.

'Why is it so cold in here?' Beth was shivering.

'Presses generate tons of heat, so they keep the place freezing. To compensate.'

She wondered how Edie knew so much.

They waited in line at the cafeteria. As it came to her turn, Beth saw that the grill man's outer forearm was marked with a blue tattooed number. She looked again. A survivor of the most terrible genocide in human history was making her grilled cheese sandwich. She felt sick with shock.

'Did you see that?' she whispered to Edie as they paid.

Edie nodded.

They took their sandwiches around the corner to the only nearby patch of green. Dealers exchanged small stacks of bills and people prepared syringes on park benches. What if her parents could see her now? She liked being part of something dirty and dangerous.

Edie wore very round, very dark sunglasses that made her look ridiculously cool. She informed Beth that she was from the Upper West Side, that she was Jewish, that she hated her name.

'Edie Gale. I mean, give me strength,' she said. 'It was Gerschkowitz until someone at Ellis Island had the great idea to change it. Gale, like gale-force wind. Not that Gerschkowitz is anything to write home about, but Gale? I never experience anything gently. My shrink says it's a self-fulfilling prophecy.'

Her shrink? 'Maybe you should change your name to something more temperate,' Beth said. 'Like Sunbeam or Zephyr.'

'Zephyr? Who's called Zephyr? That's almost as bad as Gerschkowitz. And if I was Edie Sunbeam I'd end up working in a gift shop selling flowers, imprisoned for all eternity in plastic paperweights. It would be the souvenir shop version of Sartre's *No Exit*, after two days I'd be searching the eyes of customers trying to locate my soul.'

Her patter captivated Beth. 'What about Edie Vale? Edie Glade?'

Edie snorted. 'When I do change it, I'll choose something hyper-Protestant like Quincy-Adams or Cabot-Lodge. I bet they have fewer mental health problems than Gales. Has anyone done a study on it? They definitely should. I wonder who I can talk to. NYU? Linguistics department? Psychology? Someone at the yeshiva?' Edie reached into her bag, pulled out a pack of Vantage, tapped one out and lit it. 'You want one?

Not sure I like working here, what do you think?' As she exhaled smoke, she tilted her sunglasses down and met Beth's eyes as if searching for her own answer there as well.

Beth laughed. After half a day? It seemed absurd to express an opinion so early – or at all. It hadn't occurred to her that you were even allowed an opinion, much less a negative one. 'Isn't it kind of early to tell?'

'I always make up my mind immediately. About everything. The minute I saw you I knew we'd be friends. Didn't you?'

Beth hesitated, dazed and seduced by the other girl's candour. 'No,' she said. 'I never know anything till I've thought about it practically forever.'

'That is sad. What you need are good instincts. My instincts are amazing. If I think I'm going to like someone, I'm always right. Those boys, for instance. New Wave Dan and that awful Kennebunkport preppy. I don't even have to name him Oliver Wrigglesworth cos it's already his name.'

'But …'

'I saw his application on Jeanne's desk. This job is just a technicality for him. He's going to Harvard in September, edited the *Exonian*, and his uncle's political editor of the *Washington Post*. No wonder he's so nice. I would be too if I had absolutely nothing to prove. We do not want to get friendly with his sort.'

Beth frowned. Surely Oliver was exactly the sort to get friendly with. The sort likely to end up as managing editor in a few years. She didn't understand how Edie managed to hold so many opinions so strongly. Beth didn't know what she thought until she'd considered the question at least overnight, while her brain buzzed with possibilities, alternatives, doubts.

'One thing I do think,' Beth said, 'is that nearly everyone who works here is a man. Not counting Jeanne and us. It's kind of weird.'

'Nail on the head! Too many damn men. Too many men in high places, too many men in the elevators, too many men on the third floor playing who's got the biggest dick.'

'The third floor?'

'Newsroom. Where all the big dicks live.'

Newsroom? They hadn't even been to the newsroom. 'So, uh, who does … ?' She couldn't quite bring herself to say 'dick'.

'Have the biggest dick?' Edie considered. 'Editor in Chief, of course. Publisher doesn't count. He's too big a dick to notice that anyone else even has a dick. Followed by Managing Editor. Deputy. Political editor. Business. Foreign editor. City editor. Sports kind of hovers on the outside. Whoever wins the play-offs automatically has the biggest dick. Columnists have their own dick league.'

'But—'

'Then way down at the bottom, so far down you can barely see them, like ants from an airplane, there's arts, culture, style and food. Society. Travel. The women. Not that they make less money for the paper. They probably make more. But who's got the bigger dick, Brezhnev or pesto? I ask you.'

Beth felt dizzy. 'How on earth do you know so much about newspapers? I hardly know anything.'

'Ha! Says Junior Investigative Reporter of the Year.'

'I was lucky.'

'Don't be ridiculous. No luck involved. I inherited my knowledge, which *is* luck by the way, good or bad, hard to say. Grandma's a photographer, parents met on the *Tribune*. Dad has a column in *Forbes*. Every conversation in my house is about news. Unless it's about me and why I'm such a fuck-up.'

No wonder Edie got the job. Born to it. 'What do you mean, a fuck-up?'

'Don't ask me. Ask them.' And that was the end of that conversation. 'Let's get out of here,' Edie said, as if noticing how awful the park was for the first time. 'I'd rather sit inside and freeze.'

As they left, they passed a haggard teenager,

concentrating hard on inserting a needle into the vein of one purplish arm. Her hands shook violently. Beth tried not to stare.

With lunch break over, Jeanne took them upstairs to the newsroom, the picture desk and library, back down to meet the compositors and see the presses. They began at the delivery bays where trucks delivered gigantic rolls of newsprint, saw the curved plastic plates cast from cold type laser scans, watched the page editors and typesetters at work. Three floors below reception, finished feature sections of tomorrow's paper flipped out of huge steel presses, just like in the movies.

'Just like in the movies,' said Oliver, close to her ear. The noise down here was a syncopated roar; one of the machinists shouted to the group that they'd worked here so long any dud note stood out.

'It's these guys who actually produce the paper,' Jeanne said. 'Without them there's nothing. And don't they let you know it.'

Dan led the intern pack, keen to hear everything first, scribbling notes in a reporter's notepad. He was followed by Oliver and Edie. Beth brought up the rear.

Anything you don't know, they were told, just ask.

Dan asked questions about deadlines and bylines and ethical protection of sources. Beth suspected he was showing off. She saw Jeanne's eyes narrow.

Back in the lobby, a young reporter greeted Oliver warmly. 'Catch you later for lunch,' the guy said, and Oliver explained they'd been to the same school.

When Jeanne asked if there were any questions, he caught Beth's eye and shrugged in mock despair. 'Have to borrow Dan's notes,' he said in a low voice.

At the end of the day, Beth and Edie left the building together but turned off in opposite directions, Edie to the subway, Beth to walk home. She was relieved, needing time alone to digest the onslaught of information. How on earth would she remember it all?

Dinner came from the salad bar at the Korean grocer on Broadway. The woman behind the counter weighed Beth's BBQ chicken and green salad. It came to more than she'd expected.

At home, she slid immediately into her room to avoid Dawn, ate with the box on her knees and didn't emerge till the noises in the apartment had died down. Then she sneaked out, washed her cutlery, dumped the cardboard container down the garbage chute on the landing, took a shower, brushed her teeth, ran the water till it was cool for a drink and got into bed.

It was only a little after nine, but they didn't have a TV and she felt uncomfortable walking around the Village after dark, so she read until the mosquitoes that lived in the urban jungle started buzzing around her ears. A T-shirt tied over her head didn't block out the horrible whine, so she gave up and turned off the light.

6

Beth finally encountered Tom a few mornings later, making coffee in the tiny kitchen. Why on earth would anyone do that, she wondered. It was cheap to get take-out and the stove made the apartment even hotter, something she hadn't thought possible. He looked up at her but said nothing.

'Tom?'

He nodded.

'I'm Beth.'

Tom was lanky with dark eyes and longish dark hair. 'I figured,' he said. 'How do you know Dawn?'

'Her sister was in my class,' she said. 'Did you buy another fan?'

'I will.' He was heating milk. The air in the tiny room wobbled.

'Sorry not to hang around,' she said, 'but I've got work.'

'You have a job?' He turned to look at her.

She nodded. It seemed strange that he and Dawn hadn't exchanged even basic information about her.

'What kind of work?'

'Summer intern. Newspaper.'

'Dogsbody.'

It was true that a well-trained dog might be able to do most of the running and fetching she was expected to do. She wondered what a dog would spend its salary on. Meat probably.

Tom lit a cigarette. 'You smoke?' He offered her the pack.

'I have to get dressed,' she said, and fled.

There'd been no sign of Dawn since the weekend and Beth wondered what kind of hours she kept. The bedroom door was always closed.

She examined the odd combination of new and old clothes laid out on her bed and tried mixing them to make the pathetic shortage of style go further. Instead of giving her old clothes a lift, the new clothes sank under the sheer weight of habitual wrongness. Even the striped skirt and pink T-shirt looked bad with her horrible sandals.

Beth sighed, closed her eyes, and chose.

7

The best thing about having Edie for a friend was the invincible feeling it gave her. Whatever she did with Edie was censure-exempt. Edie knew where to go, what to do, how to act, who to talk to and who to avoid. Oliver and New Wave Dan were to be shunned above all.

'Losers,' Edie said, holding her thumb and fore-finger in an L and shuddering, as if the mere thought of them was … *well*.

Beth accepted the pronouncement, rating Edie's instincts over her own. And yet. Dan's ambition annoyed her but didn't seem particularly evil. As for Oliver – she had no prior with WASPs but he always

37

looked immaculate, weatherproof and entirely at home in the world. He smelled expensive. His confidence and good manners bemused her, attracted her, made her jealous. He noticed everything, including the fact that she noticed everything too.

'Those two are exactly the wrong type,' Edie said.

But what type was that? And why were they one type, when they couldn't have been more different? Upper East Side Oliver, and Dan from a small town in Michigan. She and Edie couldn't have been more different, were they a single type? Beth had started pretending to understand things she didn't.

Edie passed a note under the partition. *Why does Jeanne dye her hair that colour?*

How can you tell she dyes her hair? Beth wrote back.

Edie appeared over the partition with a look of incredulity. 'It's as obvious as what's-his-name, the guy at reception's false teeth.'

False teeth? How did you know just by looking?

At the end of the first week, Edie announced that she'd found a new place to eat. They got sandwiches in the cafeteria as usual, took the elevator to the twelfth floor, walked through a fire door, up a further flight of steps at the very end of an unused corridor and emerged on to the roof.

The view was fantastic, across all of Midtown, down Broadway to the Village. New York looked completely different up here, a land of French chateaux in the sky.

'Don't you love water towers?' Edie asked, pointing at the ubiquitous wooden vessels-on-stilts.

'How do they work? I thought water came from pipes.'

Edie shrugged and unwrapped her second sandwich. 'No idea. They're nice though. Great place to dispose of a body.'

Not so great, Beth thought, once it started to decompose.

She was surprised at how much Edie ate. It seemed

incongruous with her childlike body. Today she seemed distracted, glum. Beth frowned at her.

'Don't mind me, it's just the old family affliction. Everyone in my family's depressed. We're all in therapy, which costs a fortune.' Edie recounted this fact blandly. 'Dr Lieb is ancient, been supporting Gales for generations.' She giggled. 'And vice versa.'

She talked about Dr Liebermann as if having a shrink was totally normal. 'He really likes me, laughs at my jokes. I've read all about transference and he's supposed to remind me of my father but he doesn't. Too old, for one thing. Too nice. I mean, sometimes he gets tough but not often. Mostly he listens and says, "Uh-huh." Occasionally he says, "Has it ever occurred to you ..." and then says something that occurred to me last century. But I like going. At least he listens.'

'How do you talk to someone twice a week for six years? Don't you run out of things to say?'

'Nah. Lately I've been telling him about you. He thinks you're good for me.'

That she could be the subject of Edie's therapy astonished Beth. 'What do you mean, good for you?'

'Isn't it obvious? You're intelligent, not a show-off. Honest, loyal and responsible.'

'Like a dog.'

Edie held up one finger. '*And* funny and smart and naturally sane. I had no chance to be naturally sane. My whole family is screwed-up. Every one of them. My shrink wants me to think of depression as a family trait, like big noses or being good at math. It helps desensitise the subject – stops it being all about my mother.'

'Your mother?'

Edie looked at her. 'Who else? Isn't your mother a freak? Mine wants to control how I look and how I think and pretty much everything I do. She totally didn't want me to take this job.' Edie's face changed when she talked about her mother.

Beth's parents were German Jews with terrible

pasts, which no one in the family ever discussed. Even her parents didn't speak about her parents.

'But the internship! You beat, like, a hundred people to get it.'

'No kidding. Other people think I'm smart. But she thinks I should branch out on my own. Stop using family connections. Like she did, right? Go into fashion or real estate. Dog training. I don't know, open a restaurant.'

'I don't see you as a dog trainer.'

'I don't like dogs. They don't like me either. I'm sure that says something important about my vibe. Like they can tell I'm unstable just by sniffing me.'

Beth considered this. 'I wonder what unstable smells like.'

'Who knows. Liquorice? Fish? Glue? Anyway, I wanted to go to Bennington but my parents said I had to stay home and go to NYU because it's cheaper but I'm sure it's so they can keep an eye on me. Not that NYU is punishment exactly, but I've spent practically every second of my life in New York City and shouldn't I get acquainted with nature someday? Also, living at home for another four years? And when you think about it, we can afford a house in East Hampton but not me going away to college? Nothing suspicious about that.'

'Do you have brothers and sisters?'

'Dad says I can bankrupt him all on my own. You?'

'One younger brother.'

'And?'

'And what?'

Edie sighed. 'Details! Everything! Aside from your fifteen minutes of fame, which everyone in America knows about. What kind of school you went to, what your parents do, what's your house like, who's your best friend, do you have a boyfriend, have you ever had sex? Jesus. Haven't you heard of conversation?'

Beth wondered if Edie had heard of conversation. It seemed more like an interrogation, though she didn't really mind being swept along by the force of Edie's personality. She liked being swept along.

'I'm from Providence. The suburbs. My parents are teachers. House? Nothing special. Front yard, back yard. Apple tree. Lawn.'

Edie made impatient hand movements.

'My best friend is Rachel.' She stopped.

'Go on, go on.'

'She's on an exchange programme in Greece and I'm living in the Village with her sister and her sister's boyfriend. They're older. I never met them till now.'

'Huh,' Edie said. 'Are they awful? What's the sister like? Noisy sex?'

'Sort of loud. Not loud sex, at least not that I've noticed. The place is unbearably hot. Like an oven. Rachel's sister calls it a fucking slum.'

'OK.' Edie listened hard, like she was committing the conversation to memory.

'What else did you ask? School? Well, you kind of

know about my school. Shady dealings and illegal quotas on undesirables. Boyfriend, not really.'

'Sex?'

'Um …' Beth feigned nonchalance. 'Not really.'

'Not really, not really. What does that mean?'

'Well, some sex but not, um …'

'Full penetration?' Edie huffed. 'I'm going to call that technically no sex.'

'Fine. But—'

'Now in contrast, I've had lots of sex,' Edie said. 'In my experience it's not all that great. Foreplay sure. Endless promise for the rest, good in parts, disappointing at the finish. If you know what I mean.'

Beth was struggling to keep up. 'Not …'

'But who knows if that's an observation applicable to the general public or just to me.'

'I guess it would be …'

'Have you discovered the book room?' Edie asked.

Beth shook her head, dazzled by the conversation's hairpin turns.

'Follow me.'

Edie jumped up and Beth followed her in from the roof, down endless fire escape stairs to the fourth floor. How did she know her way around the building so well? Beth was still going the wrong way to the bathroom.

Edie was sweetness and light with the guy at reception, asking for keys to the book room with a winning smile. He handed them over without seeming to notice.

'Be nice to everyone,' Edie whispered. 'You never know who might come in handy.'

Beth nodded.

Edie unlocked the closet door and switched on the light. It flickered to life, revealing five by five feet of books crammed three or four deep on floor-to-ceiling metal shelves. The whole construction looked precarious in the extreme.

'Go on,' hissed Edie. 'Choose some.'

Beth scanned one wall in a panic of desire. There were bestsellers, recent releases, reissues of classics, art books, science books, anything you could think of. She looked at Edie. 'Are you sure this is OK?'

'Sure. Just hurry, they don't like people hanging around forever. Interns especially.'

Beth chose a few novels and Edie stuffed them into her bag. She scanned the shelves till she found a recently published portfolio of Ansel Adams photographs.

'My grandma will like this. She's eighty-six.' She turned off the light, locked the door and handed the key back to reception. When they were out of ear-shot, she said, 'Pretty good, huh?'

'How'd you even know it was there?'

'The guy in the library told me. Amazing what people reveal if you talk to them.'

'Like what?'

'Like "What's the best thing about working here?"'

or "What happens on those upper floors?" It's not that hard. People get bored doing their jobs every day. They want someone to ask questions.' She turned and looked at Beth. 'It's your *responsibility*. How else will you learn?'

What Edie was somehow leaving out of the equation were the intangibles – smile/haircut/clothes/body/manner. *If I looked like Edie*, Beth thought, *I'd be socially fearless too.*

'My mantra is, you have to start somewhere. Remember that. Sew it on a sampler. I always dive in because, and this is key, they are not judging you,' Edie said. 'That's the secret. They're never thinking about you. They're thinking about them.'

8

Some girls looked fantastic in hot weather. Some developed a sprinkling of freckles and a tawny glow across the bridge of their nose and cheekbones. Their breasts stayed up without a bra; sundresses flowed around their bodies like smoke. They had delicate feet that slipped gracefully into sandals and hair that pulled up into ponytails – thick, handsome and cool. Their lips held a slick of lipstick for hours, or better yet, had enough natural colour to render make-up unnecessary. They had waists that invited belts and skin that always glowed.

Beth was not one of those girls.

Make-up slipped off her face like oil off hot

chrome. Her hair, thick and curly in winter, turned to frizz when the humidity rose. Her breasts were the wrong shape to resist gravity and she chewed her nails unattractively to stubs. She never picked up a pen without knowing that ink would eventually leak out on to her hands or the back pocket of her jeans. And no matter how often she showered, she never had that pristine look that some women seemed born with.

At least the office was freezing.

Edie was pretty in the near-death way that was just starting to gain traction in magazines and rock bands: large eyes, small face, equal parts fragile and bold. She looked young, but there was a weariness in her demeanour that made bartenders pause before carding her. She was always carded anyway, mainly as an excuse, Beth thought. No one cared how old she was.

It helped that she made you think she looked great even when she didn't. She'd recently taken to wearing a red wool beret all day in the cold office and on her it looked like radical chic, like she was just back from a Black Panthers demo or the Spanish Civil War.

Bob on the picture desk gave her a thumbs-up. 'Be my Guardian Angel,' he called, referencing the vigilantes in red berets who patrolled the subways.

Beth spent her waking hours trying to unlock the secret of her friend's confidence. Edie dressed well as if dressing well were as simple as breathing. She talked as if everyone wanted to hear what she had to say. She outlined her gigantic eyes with black kohl but never seemed to care how she looked.

Fashion confused Beth. Style was something French women had.

Edie knew what looked good on her, recognised superior quality and knew where to find it. Second-hand clothes barely existed as a concept in New York, but Edie said she'd rather wear second-hand designer than first-hand Gap. So, after work one day she dragged Beth to her favourite place on Lower Fifth, and while Beth stared in hopeless confusion at rack after crammed rack of clothes on commission, Edie popped up in front of the mirror in a short silver leather biker jacket that looked like a million dollars.

'That's because it probably was,' she said, showing Beth the label. *Chanel*, it read, in elegant sans serif. Edie dropped her voice. 'It's the real thing. Someone paid a fortune for this and inexplicably tired of it. She must have died. There's no other explanation.'

Having paid (very little) for the jacket, Edie dedicated herself to finding something for Beth, eventually pulling out a long linen jacket with shoulder pads, and two short flippy silk skirts that appeared to be new. Beth wouldn't have dreamed of putting them together, but it worked – Edwardian gentleman meets Josephine Baker, Edie said.

'Who's Josephine Baker?' Beth twisted in front of the mirror, trying to see the back of her outfit.

Edie rolled her eyes.

'I think I like it,' Beth said.

'Excellent. You should always wear long jackets and short skirts. It's your look.'

Beth, sweating and red-faced in the tiny window-less dressing room, liked having a look.

'Now what you need is a haircut,' Edie said. 'We can go to training night at the Fashion Institute where they'll do it for free. If you go on Tuesdays, you get the teachers instead of the students. And they do all sorts of great stuff.'

Beth looked worried.

'Rejoice,' commanded Edie. 'Everyone in New York is getting a perm and you don't need one.'

Beth hated her hair. How could she not, when everyone gorgeous looked like Cher. But when she and Edie arrived, the students buzzed with excitement. She kept her eyes shut through the operation, which took much longer than an ordinary haircut, as the instructor explained every cut he made. When at last it was finished, he took four Polaroids, one from each side, and pronounced that she looked like a French film star.

'There,' Edie said. 'You don't look like a girl from the suburbs anymore.' Which was great, because not-a-girl-from-the-suburbs was exactly the look she was after. The students gathered around, comparing Before and After photos which were then pinned to the wall.

Now when they went out together, Beth felt less like some sort of shabby hanger-on.

A well-dressed woman stopped her on the street a few days later. 'I'm sorry to bother you,' she said, 'but could you tell me who cuts your hair?'

Which may well have been the best moment of her life.

9

A daily paper was always busy, and interns mopped up the work no one else wanted to do. Gofers, runners and copy boys fetched stationery from the supply cupboard, cleared up after meetings, made coffee and unjammed Xerox machines. Beth had great instincts for what needed doing, while Edie always knew how to get it done or who to ask for help. She found her way around the newspaper as if she'd been born there, which in a way she had.

'It's logical,' she said. 'You can't have advertising a million miles away from sales promotion. And news-rooms all look the same. Copy-editors, sub-editors, fact checkers, big dick in the moral centre, think of a model of the solar system. Planets revolve around the sun.'

Day by day and detail by detail, Beth began to grasp the intricacies of the job. If someone asked for files on Imelda Marcos, you had to narrow the request as much as possible, otherwise you'd end up with too much information and more clipping files than you could carry. Edie discovered that you didn't need a job number to order copies of any photograph the paper had on file and snuck her own requests in with her work.

'Don't hide in your cubicle,' she instructed.

Obediently, Beth took to seeking out odd jobs, returning stacked files to the library, carrying messages from one department to another.

She ran into Oliver coming out of the photo library and they walked back to their floor together. He no longer dressed in suits but his chinos were immaculate and he always wore a tie. For a moment she couldn't remember why they weren't supposed to be friends, except perhaps that he made her feel conspicuously Jewish, a social divide that could never be crossed. Edie didn't look particularly Jewish, and if you didn't know about her shrink and her many neuroses, you might not have guessed.

Beth could imagine Oliver's father working at some very old law firm where they didn't hire Jews or Black people, not so much out of policy as tradition.

'How's it going, Beth?'

'OK. No one's suggested I leave. I guess that's a good sign?'

'Very good sign.' He veered left at the top of the stairs. 'Coffee?'

'Oh, yes please. I hate this time of the morning. I'm starving and it's ages till lunch.'

Oliver made two cups of coffee in the tiny kitchen and passed her one.

'Thanks.' Beth took a handful of Half-and-Halfs and four sugars, emptying them one by one into her cup.

Oliver winced. 'Oh good Lord, please stop.'

'You should try it,' Beth said, gulping it down. 'It's kind of like a coffee milkshake. Surprisingly delicious.'

'And so sophisticated.' Oliver sipped his black coffee. 'Are you liking features?'

'More to the point, are you liking news? Do you think the assignments have anything to do with the fact that we're girls and you're not? All those wars and international treaties on your side. All those recipes and sun hats on ours.'

Oliver laughed. 'Woman's work.'

Beth joined in a bit uneasily.

'Better go,' Oliver said. 'International treaties call.'

'Ditto, sun hats. Thanks again for the coffee.'

He paused. 'Dan and I are going to the City Bar after work if you and your sidekick want to join us.'

Edie wouldn't like that. 'Busy tonight. Really sorry, Oliver.' She was. 'Another time?'

On their way out of the building that night, she told Edie about the invitation. Edie stopped. 'Wait, you don't actually *like* like him, do you? He's gay as confetti. You mean you didn't notice?' She gave Beth a pitying look. 'Don't worry, lots of women don't have the instinct.'

Beth felt ashamed but tried not to show it.

10

Dawn bought an old Oriental rug at the flea market on 25th and covered the living-room floor.

Tom looked thoughtful. 'Why do you suppose they call it a "flea" market?'

'They swore it was flea-free,' said Dawn.

'I'm positive those people you'll never see again wouldn't lie to you.'

Dawn ignored him.

'Assuming there are fleas,' he continued, 'we'll never get rid of them. They're the only creatures to have survived Hiroshima.'

'Really?' Beth was genuinely curious. 'Fleas? Are you sure?'

'He makes shit up,' Dawn said. 'Ignore him.'

Tom glanced at Beth and raised an eyebrow. 'Totally sure.'

Dawn huffed. She used her parents' credit card to buy pillows and posters from Village headshops. On garbage days, Tom scavenged, rising at six to comb surrounding blocks for discarded treasure. Today, he brought back a large Chinese bowl with a hairline crack. Beth thought it was beautiful.

'It's my gift from the universe,' Dawn said, picking it up and examining it, 'to celebrate getting a job.'

'Your gift?' Tom frowned. 'I found it.'

'But who found the job?'

'Totally irrelevant. Give it back.'

Dawn tossed it more or less in his direction and he lunged to catch it. 'Don't treat my stuff like garbage,' he said, furious.

Dawn shrugged. 'Garbage in, garbage out.'

'Hang on, you got a job?' Beth said. 'That's great.'

'Yup. Bartender. At that new place on Bleecker,

the Italian with the big paintings of flowers in the window. I barely had to interview. They just wanted someone who looks good.' She struck a pose. 'No-brainer. I'm doing nights, six to two. Sorry, Tom.' She leaned over to kiss him, but he shrank away.

Did Dawn look good? Her chin seemed too small for her face, which made her teeth stick out. She had straight blonde hair held back with a college-girl velvet hairband. Her chest was big and her face had a permanent glower. Beth wondered what had attracted Tom. It seemed unlikely to be her personality.

Beth couldn't figure out what Tom was doing here. He and Dawn didn't seem particularly inter-ested in each other. Dawn said they'd been together since freshman year, in what Beth thought might be just a bad habit. Tom frequently expressed annoy-ance when Dawn spoke, though she never seemed to notice. Why would he stick around if he didn't like her? Why would she want him to? Beth guessed that at least part of it was practical. It helped having someone to share the rent.

Tom worked at a deli uptown called Chiasso, where only bankers and movie stars shopped. He said people ran up weekly accounts of hundreds of dollars buying three meals a day and sent their assistants in to pay at the end of the week. Tom brought home the stuff they'd paid for and not bothered to pick up, like ravioli with truffles and lemon mousse cake. Chiasso had a policy of throwing out all prepared food at the end of the day. If it was too small to slice but perfectly good to eat, it went to staff. A butt end of something delicious like Parma ham or spiced pastrami, a piece of Gorgonzola cut the wrong size or a ciabatta that wouldn't live to see tomorrow all found their way into his daily bag. Staff were supposed to pay a nominal price for swag, but never did.

'Hey, Tom. What you got?' Beth had arrived home just before him.

'Nothing.'

'Come on. Show me.' She tried to peer into the heavy white Chiasso bag.

'Hands off. Porcini risotto. Out of your league.'

'Yum,' she said.

The way Tom spoke to her was puzzling. Older brother, maybe, but was he flirting? It was impossible to know. His way of speaking was so odd, she couldn't figure out whether he genuinely liked her company or genuinely didn't care.

If Tom didn't show up with dinner, Beth bought salad from the Korean grocer. It was too hot to cook, even if any of them had known how. When Dawn wasn't home, Beth occasionally kept him company on the fire escape. Occasionally he'd rest his hand on her leg, as casually as if she were a radiator. Just as casually, she'd remove it; he barely seemed to notice.

A couple of days after Dawn started her new job, Beth came home to find Tom moping.

'Still here?' she said.

'I'm here, but where's my so-called girlfriend? At work as usual. I sometimes think I miss her, but when she's here, I always wish she were somewhere else.'

'Aren't you supposed to like the person you're dating?'

'I guess.' Tom pulled a piece of apricot custard tart out of his bag and handed it to Beth.

'Thanks. Not to change the subject, but has anyone dared open the fridge?'

'Yeah,' Tom said. 'It's OK in there. A little mouldy but we wiped it.'

Beth blinked. *Wiped?*

'There's cold water in a bottle.'

She opened the door cautiously. It was a heavy, old-fashioned fridge, large enough for a Thanksgiving turkey and ten pounds of potatoes, with nothing inside but a bottle of water and half a lime. Beth poured cold water into a glass.

'It's too fucking hot in here,' Tom said. 'I can't stand it. Let's go somewhere air-conditioned.'

'I'm a bit …' She didn't like to say broke, but she was. They hadn't been paid yet.

'I'll pay,' he said.

'Don't be stupid. You're not exactly raking it in.'

'I have a trust fund,' he said gloomily.

'You actually do?'

'Yes.' He sighed. 'No, just kidding. Come on. We'll go someplace cheap.'

'OK.' Anything to get out of this sweat box.

They went to a no-frills Thai place around the corner and got a table for two. The waiter appeared before they'd picked up their menus. Quick service, freezing temperatures. Maximum turnover.

'Two red curry noodle soups,' Tom said, and turned to her. 'That OK? Lots of chilli. Keeps you cool.'

She nodded.

'Plus, it's the best thing on the menu. You want a beer?'

She shook her head.

'Two Thai beers,' he said to the waiter, and to Beth, 'I'll drink yours.'

The waiter went away leaving an awkward silence.

'You're great company,' he said.

'Thanks.'

'Ever heard of small talk?'

'Small talk?' She frowned at him. 'What are you, my great-aunt?'

He looked glum and said nothing for a long moment. 'Barely July and already I'm having the worst summer of my life.'

Then his hand was on her arm. She stared at it.

'How come you haven't got a boyfriend?'

'Too ugly, obviously.'

'You're not bad-looking.'

She moved her arm. 'Wow, that's pretty much the nicest thing anyone's ever said to me.'

'Yeah, well.' He shook his head. 'God, women are complicated.'

'What, all of them? All women?'

'You know what I mean.'

Their food arrived.

'No, I don't,' she said. 'Why don't you do something about your dead-end relationship instead of complaining that all women are the problem.'

'You mean break up with Dawn?'

She put down her spoon. 'I don't know, Tom. I don't know anything about you. But it's a thought, surely. You two aren't exactly couple of the year.'

'I didn't bring you here for advice. I brought you for the air-con.'

'It's not advice, it's just idle observation. I'm telling you what I see. And it's enough to put anyone off ever having a relationship. With anyone. Ever.'

'OK. Sorry I spoke.'

They ate in silence for a few minutes.

Beth gave in. 'Why is this the worst summer of your life?'

'Isn't it obvious?'

'Not to me.'

'I can't explain. We'd be here all night.' He slurped his noodles loudly. It was annoying.

She stared at him and he stopped.

He frowned. 'You eighteen?'

'Yes.'

'Going to college in September?'

'Uh-huh.'

'So, this is the first time you've lived away? First day of the rest of your life. Sex with whoever you want. Bet you feel old.'

'Ancient.'

'You better find a boyfriend soon. Get yourself some action.'

Beth put down her spoon and stood up. 'Thanks for dinner, Tom. I'm going home.'

'Joke!'

She didn't even feel particularly angry, just chilled and sweaty and exasperated. Tom drove her insane. Sometimes he was fine, nice even, but most of the time he was an asshole.

She arrived home tired and sweaty, trudged up the stairs, unlocked the door and turned on her fan in a futile attempt to budge the near-solid volume of heat. After a cool shower she began to feel shivery, took the last two aspirin in the bottle and went to bed, waking from a heavy feverish sleep sometime later to what sounded like tapping on her bedroom door. She wasn't sure whether she was awake or asleep, but either way, she ignored it and it stopped.

11

The fever had full hold of her by five the next morning. She woke up shivering with steam rising from her skin, desperate to get cool and warm at once. Her feet were cold, her head hot and stuffed with straw. Dreams hallucinated their way into real time so she couldn't tell if she was asleep, awake, or floating in limbo. Her body hovered up near the ceiling. She hoped Tom or Dawn would come in to see why she hadn't gone to work, but they didn't, and by supreme force of will she managed to crawl to the telephone and inform Jeanne that she wasn't coming in.

'You don't sound good,' Jeanne said. 'Take some aspirin and stay in bed.'

She poured a glass of water and went back to bed with the fan blowing directly at her face but periodically had to pull socks and a sweatshirt on to stop the shivering. Ten minutes later it was wet towels again to quench her burning chest.

On her way to the bathroom, she ran into Dawn.

'Holy shit, what's wrong? You look fucking terrible.'

'I know.'

'Hope I don't get it. I'll get you something, some ... What do you want?'

'Only if you're going out. Orange juice maybe? And more aspirin.'

'Christ,' Dawn said. 'Your pyjamas are soaked – don't you have another pair?' Dawn rummaged around in her room and came back with a Snoopy sleep shirt. 'Take this. At least it's dry.'

The day passed in a kaleidoscope of fractured

dreams. She woke in a desperate state, hot, dehydrated and urgently thirsty but too weak even to reach down for the glass by the bed. Her skin hurt and her bones ached with cold. Another time-slip and her limbs were too heavy to move, her dreams psychedelic. In one dream, Tom was laying cool hands on her skin.

Tom was laying cool hands on her skin. 'Shall I call your parents?' he asked. 'You're boiling hot and I'd hate for you to die alone.'

'I'm not dying.' Her voice was barely a whisper. Why couldn't he be serious even for a second?

'Maybe not, but you can never be sure. Is your neck stiff? Does the light sear your eyeballs? Are you scared of water?'

'No,' she said.

'Not rabies then,' he said. 'Or meningitis. Go back to sleep. If you're not better in a day or two, I'll call someone. A medic. A witch-doctor.'

She closed her eyes, but her eyeballs grated against

the lids and ached so much she opened them again. 'Could you get me some ice if we have any? Please? And aspirin?'

He brought her the contents of an entire tray of ice cubes wrapped in one of his T-shirts and proceeded to smash it against the floor.

'Tom, *please*.' The noise made her head clang with pain.

'Sorry,' he whispered. 'Just trying to crush the cubes. Here.' He handed her the ice, two aspirin and a glass of water.

'Thank you.' The ice quenched the fire in her head and she sighed with relief. It felt wonderful until the heat of the room and her skin turned it into a clammy puddle on her bed.

The following morning at eleven, the phone rang. Incapable of getting up, she imagined drifting across the room to answer it. Who could it be? Had her parents got wind of the fact that she was at death's door? She imagined a doctor asking, 'Can you still feel your hands?' After a long time, the ringing stopped.

At intervals she sipped tepid orange juice, the glass topped with a book to stop cockroaches swimming in it. When it ran out, she walked slowly to the kitchen for water, swaying and holding on to the wall for support.

The phone rang again and she picked it up. 'Hello,' she croaked.

'Wow,' said the voice at the other end. 'You sound terrible.'

Terrible seemed to be something everyone could agree on. 'Hey, Edie. How's work?'

'Missing you, that's for sure. Some guy on the city desk asked me out for a drink. Do you think I should go?'

'Which one?'

'The kind of good-looking one I did the photo search for last week.'

'He's got to be forty.'

'Sure, but a date's a date. I don't get asked out much.'

Beth groaned. 'I don't care what you do. I'm way too sick to care.'

'I'm glad you're alive,' Edie said. 'Can I come visit tomorrow? After work?'

Her head ached. 'I don't know. It's too hot. Can we talk in the morning?'

'Sure. Feel better.'

A few hours later Dawn stuck her head into the room. 'I'm going out. You want something? Jello? Ice cream? What do sick people like?'

The pain in her chest made swallowing difficult. And she wasn't hungry. 'Ice cream maybe. Thank you. You want some … ?' She scrambled around feebly for her wallet.

Dawn waved. 'Go back to bed.'

When Beth woke it was dark and her head ached less than before. The apartment was sweltering. She turned the fan back on, shuffled through to the kitchen and checked the freezer. Caramel Swirl ice cream was shoved into a small cavern in the frost. Groaning, she leaned her head into the compartment, imagined crawling in or having a freezer big enough to accommodate her whole body. She took the carton back to bed, pressing it on her burning face and chest to soften it. Although only able to manage a few spoonfuls, it tasted delicious. When she woke again at 2 a.m., the liquid remains of the ice cream beside her bed were swarming with cockroaches. Thousands of them. She felt like screaming but instead sobbed and sobbed until, exhausted, she fell asleep.

Later that morning, she got a garbage bag from the kitchen and used it to pick up the leftover ice cream, wanting to throw up as she knotted the top so its inhabitants couldn't escape, stuffed it down the garbage chute and hoped never to have to think of it again.

The effort exhausted her and she slept on and off

in a fog of peculiar visions, cockroaches and night-marish images from her job, people shouting that she'd ruined everything, her parents saying she was too young to leave home, a train crash, the cars split open with insects pouring from them. She woke up mid-afternoon, sweating and thoroughly uncomfort-able, her bed damp, her sheets grubby. But the fever was gone. When Edie called she told her to come after work.

Beth showered and dressed in a loose shirt, stripped the sheets off her bed and remade it. Air from the fan gave the illusion of a breeze. She felt human for the first time in days.

Edie arrived wearing her wool beret in the searing heat as a statement of corporeal indifference. She lugged a Zabar's bag, which she unpacked on to the coffee table: a cardboard container of matzoh ball soup, a corned beef sandwich, two bottles of seltzer, a jar of half-sour pickles, half a dozen bagels, some cream cheese and a large carton of cut fruit.

'It's a mixed bag,' Edie said from the wooden folding chair. She took in the room with a blank expression.

'No, this is amazing,' Beth croaked. 'There's way too much food but I'm starving. You have some.' Edie took half the corned beef sandwich.

The salty crunch of a half-sour pickle sent Beth into a kind of ecstasy. If you didn't eat for days, food tasted psychedelic.

Edie moved on to the tiny sofa next to Beth and told her about her date with the guy from the city desk. 'We practically had sex in the bar,' she said. 'He was ridiculously up for it, but then it turns out he has a pregnant wife, and that put me off.'

'Don't know why. Edie, please sit over there. It's too hot to be near you.'

'Don't push me away. I need love.' She tried to snuggle up and put her head on her friend's shoulder.

Beth pushed her off, and with a sigh, Edie

relocated to the folding chair. 'I'm way too sick to give love,' Beth said. 'Is he even nice?'

'Nice?' Edie thought about it. 'How nice can he be, having sex in a bar with me while his pregnant wife's at home? Anyway, it's hard to measure nice-ness when someone's really interested in you. They seem nice because they want to buy you drinks and have sex with you. That in itself is nice.'

She had a point.

Tom arrived half an hour later and Edie offered him the other half of her sandwich.

'Oh God, no.'

'No offence, Tom works in a deli,' Beth said. 'Ital-ian, but still.'

Edie nodded. 'I should go, but maybe see you tomorrow? It's totally awful without you. No one to talk to except Oliver and New Wave Dan. And pregnant-wife guy. But maybe I won't talk to him anymore if you disapprove. I'm not doing anything you disapprove of ever again. Starting today.'

Beth rolled her eyes. 'Ow,' she said, because it hurt. 'Don't be weird.'

'I'll try. I want you to be proud of me.'

'You're screwing with my head and I'm too sick to cope. Go home.'

'OK. Wait, I have a card for you.'

'A card?'

'Someone left it on my desk. Open it, who's it from?'

Beth opened the envelope, on which her name was written, and pulled out the card. It was made from folded copy paper. On the front was a drawing of a red heart with a thermometer run through it like an arrow. Inside it just said *Get better*, and was signed with an 'O'. Oliver. Her own heart flickered.

Edie shook her head. 'So inappropriate.'

'Go home.' Beth pointed at the door.

'Yes, OK, OK. Get better soon. I'll call you tomorrow.'

'Thanks for the food.'

'Sure.'

'And thank Oliver for me.'

'Gay Oliver.'

'Go!'

Drained by the visit, Beth put everything in the fridge and went back to bed. After a while Tom knocked on her bedroom door, came in and sat on the bed.

'What's up with your friend? She's kind of strange.'

'Nothing's up.'

'She's cool though. Something about her.'

'You could hit on her. Your girlfriend won't mind.'

'I haven't seen my girlfriend in like a week.'

'That must be devastating for you.'

'It is.'

'You think she's trying to tell you something by working nights?'

'Maybe. Hey, you look better.' He put a hand on her forehead. 'How's this supposed to feel?'

'Go away, Tom. I need sleep.'

'You want anything?'

'No.' And then, nicer, 'Thanks.' He was a jerk, but she was pretty sure he didn't mean to be.

He went out. She turned her fan to face the bed and fell into a deep sleep.

12

Edie called the following lunchtime.

'I'm not coming in today,' Beth said. 'I got up, had a shower and felt so bad I went back to bed. Jeanne was nice but I feel really guilty. Worst intern ever.'

'I didn't call about work. I called to see if you want to come stay at my place. It's way nicer than yours and air-conditioned. I'm on my own for the summer and company would be amazing.'

'You think my place is a slum.'

'Obviously. No offence. So, what do you think? I've got plenty of room.'

Beth's instinct was to say *No, I couldn't possibly accept, but thank you very much for offering.* 'Wait, is this a real offer? For the whole summer? Are you serious?'

'Totally.'

'But what about your parents?'

'They're in East Hampton. They'll be there till September. And they'll like that I have company. My mother's always going on about how I don't have enough friends.'

'God, she sounds horrible.'

'You have no idea.'

Beth hesitated. Was she allowed to say yes? No money had been mentioned. Would she be expected to pay? If not, it was too big a favour. But …

'I could give you my salary for rent.'

'Don't be stupid. I don't want any rent. I don't pay any.'

Beth was silent.

'Don't you want to come?'

'Of course I want to come. But it seems like such an imposition. How could I ever pay you back?'

'Just stop talking, hang up the phone, pack your bag and come up tonight. Really. Let's stop discussing it.'

'What if we don't get along?'

'We do get along, that's the whole point. Do you think I'd ask you to move in if we didn't get along?'

'Wow. Wow. I mean, thank you. Look, if it doesn't work out, you can always ask me to—'

'For Christ's sake, Beth. Now look, a taxi seems expensive but get one. No way should you be on public transport in your condition.'

'*In my condition*? What am I, pregnant?'

'Are you paying attention?'

'Yes. OK.'

'So, I'll see you later? After work? I'll leave early.'

'OK, yes. Thank you.'

'Here's the address.' Beth scribbled it down. 'And get a cab. Promise?'

'Promise. Thank you. Thank you.'

Beth hung up. Across the room she could see a

cockroach climbing the wall. Living in this apartment was bad enough; having the flu in it was monstrous.

Edie's offer felt like the commutation of a jail sentence. She imagined living on the Upper West Side with her new best friend. And air conditioning. Everyone said the heat was going to last for weeks.

She took her time packing, stuffing dirty sheets and towels into the bottom drawer of the dresser. Without them, there was room for the things she'd bought new. She washed Dawn's Snoopy shirt and hung it up in the shower. It would dry in minutes. Then, with the last of her energy, she swept the floor in case they wanted to rent the room to someone else and left a note for Dawn with a cheque, saying she'd still cover her half of the rent. For a few seconds she considered leaving Tom a P.S. but couldn't think what to say.

By the time she hauled her suitcase downstairs she was aching, drenched and starting to shiver again, despite the thick air. She hailed a cab but didn't dare look at the meter.

Northwest corner, Edie had said. She understood corners now. The cab was expensive and the cabbie didn't help with her bag. Her clothes stuck to her skin and her hairline dripped, but the lobby was cool and elegant with big comfortable chairs and mirrors everywhere. The doorman called up to Edie and carried Beth's bag to the elevator. She felt ashamed by how shabby and ill she looked, and wondered if she was supposed to tip him.

'Thank you,' she said instead, and he reached inside to press the button for the twelfth floor.

The elevator opened and Edie was there, apartment door open, saying '*Come in!*' and grabbing her bag.

'Ta-da!' she said, throwing one arm out as welcome. '*Mi casa es su casa.*'

Beth almost couldn't believe it. The entrance to Edie's apartment was tiled in grey marble with a slate-topped console table on which two antique cameras sat mounted on wooden plinths like works of art. It felt like a place that grown-up people lived, a real place, not some horrible tenement inhabited by students because it was all they could afford. Everything about it was quiet, elegant and calm. The views out the windows were amazing, of trees and building tops, and busy streets and brownstones down below. And best of all it was actually cool, with air conditioners humming away in every window. Beth began to cry.

Edie put the bag down. 'Oh, don't,' she said and hugged her. 'Come on, here's your room.' She led her halfway down the hall and opened the door to a square bedroom with cream wool carpet, black-and-white framed photographs covering every wall, and a high, old-fashioned double bed made up with white sheets.

Beth tiptoed in, unable to believe her change in fortune.

'Are you hungry?'

'Just thirsty.' Tears continued to spill out of her eyes. 'Oh God, Edie, thank you so much for letting me stay. I'm so happy to be here, I'll be grateful for the rest of my life.'

'Wow, that's a long time.'

'I mean it. You saved me.'

'I did. But it's great for me too. I hate being alone.' Edie went out and came back with a tall glass of seltzer and ice in which a slice of lime floated. It was the lime that made Beth cry again.

'You're so good to me. But would you mind if I went to bed? I feel unbearably happy but everything hurts.'

Edie shook her head. 'There's aspirin in the bathroom. You need anything else, just call.' She waved and closed the door.

The room had its own bathroom, which was also white. All Beth's resolve, all her courage in the face of adversity and illness fell away, leaving her wobbly as an oyster. She cried helplessly, with a childish combination of self-pity and relief. It was only 6 p.m., but she had a shower, turned the air conditioner down to night mode, dug out a clean T-shirt, climbed into the cool bed, turned out the lights and fell instantly asleep.

Fourteen hours later, Edie stuck her head in. 'Morning, Sunshine!'

Beth groaned. 'What day is it?'

'Saturday. Jeanne wants me to come in for a few hours. I'll be back around lunchtime. Help yourself to breakfast and anything else you want.' And she was gone.

The whole grubby feeling of Beth's illness – her sweaty clothes, the Village apartment, the cockroaches – fell away. She stumbled out of bed, made her way to the kitchen and poured a glass of cold grapefruit juice from the spotless fridge. No cockroaches scuttled on the surfaces or scurried up the walls, though she still imagined them in her peripheral vision.

Her face was less swollen. Her joints ached hardly at all. One more day and she'd be back to normal.

Padding around the pristine apartment, she peered into Edie's parents' bedroom, with its white Moroccan rug, dark brown leather headboard and matching side tables. She scanned through the books in the living room, examined the collection of mounted pre-Columbian figures along the tops of the bookcases, sat in one of the white leather-and-chrome Barcelona chairs, and then went back to bed and dozed. It was easy to forget the stinking garbage and noisy streets of Greenwich Village up here. Up here was a whole different New York, one with trees, doormen and air conditioning. The difference was money. Money made everything better.

Edie returned at two with hot-and-sour soup, moo shu pork and dry-fried green beans from the Chinese on Broadway, because, she said, spicy food would be therapeutic. Therapeutic or not, it was delicious.

Beth sipped hot-and-sour soup and thanked Edie again for saving her life, and then asked about her grandmother, whose photographs hung on every wall of the apartment.

She was still very much alive, Edie said, and living in an artists' colony in the West Village. Still taking pictures. 'You have to meet her. She's amazing. Thank God someone in my family is. Here, have some pork.'

'God, I love pork,' Beth said, 'though my parents would kill me.'

Edie said it figured that Jews weren't allowed pork: what else would you expect from a jealous and vindictive God?

Before they'd even finished, Edie broke out the fortune cookies. 'I hope mine says I'll be lucky in love,' she said, cracking it in two. 'Let's see. *Observe everything, but most of all yourself.* What does that mean? Totally inscrutable. I must have opened yours by mistake.'

'Hey!' Beth said, as Edie tried to snatch her cookie. 'Oh this is wise. *Every stranger is a friend you haven't met.*'

'Hmm.' Edie paused. 'Speaking of friends you haven't met, do you want to hear about Mike? The guy from the city desk?'

'Do I have to?' Beth crunched her cookie.

'That's the only rule of living with me. You have to listen to my problems and give advice. I'm impetuous and you're sensible. That's why we get along.'

Beth sighed. 'Fine.'

'So we went on this date. Not a date. To a bar.'

'The one you almost had sex in.'

'That's it. In Chelsea.'

'Of course. He doesn't want to be seen near work with an intern young enough to be his daughter, what with the preg—'

Edie glared. 'Once we got there we just talked and talked, like we knew each other forever. It was intense.'

'Did you drink and drink or just talk and talk?'

'Drank and drank. But that wasn't why. He's really smart and not at all stuck up.'

'Uh-huh.'

'And God is he sexy. I mean, I couldn't keep my hands off him.'

'After how many drinks?'

'It wasn't the alcohol.'

'For God's sake, Edie. The guy's wife is having a baby and you can't keep your hands off him? How is this going to end well? I don't care about him. He sounds like a total loser—'

'He's *not* a loser.'

'He *sounds* like a loser. Maybe he is, maybe he's not. It doesn't matter what he is. It'll end with him walking away and you getting hurt and you'll wonder why you ever thought this was a good idea in the first place.'

Edie sat for a moment looking glum. 'That's not what I want to hear.'

'Wait, so my job is to listen and give advice, but only advice you want to hear?'

Edie's face brightened. 'That's it! Now have some more food and stop preaching. You're totally right but I can't help what I am.'

'Edie, you're gorgeous. You could attract anyone. Why go for him?'

'I'm self-destructive. That's what Dr Lieb says anyway.'

Her matter-of-fact tone annoyed Beth. 'Well, if you know what you are, can't you make the tiniest effort to fix it? You know exactly where this relationship's going, so just—'

'I'm also desperate for love.' Edie sighed. 'It's a tragic duality.'

Beth laughed. 'OK, have your tragic duality. I'm finishing the pork.'

Between them they finished everything. Then they walked around the neighbourhood slowly, till they couldn't stand the heat another second, retreated to the air conditioning, found a bad movie on TV, made popcorn, and talked about Edie's love life till it was time for bed.

Edie left early on Sunday morning to see her grandma, and Beth was only just getting up when she arrived back with a bag of bagels and a dozen eggs for brunch. It felt like waking up in heaven.

Beth had never met anyone so open about what Edie called her *issues* – but then she didn't know anyone who had a therapist, much less anyone who talked about having a therapist. It struck her as very New York, and therefore very sophisticated, to be so forthcoming about one's flaws. In the suburbs, everyone pretended to be fine, disguising drug addiction, infidelity and mental illness behind closed doors and lawn ornaments.

Beth felt like a sparrow or a squirrel, something dull and ordinary that had somehow wandered into this glorious lair with its exotic inhabitant. Yet Edie seemed as happy about her presence as Beth was for her change of circumstance.

She thought about it for a long time and decided at last that the best course of action was to stop feeling guilty and appreciate her extravagant luck.

13

Jeanne welcomed Beth back to work on Monday with customary effusiveness. 'It's good you're better,' she said. 'Work's backing up.'

Oliver and Dan came by with coffee.

'Wow, you look bad,' Dan said.

'Stick-thin,' said Oliver.

'Consumptive.'

'Death's door.'

'Thanks,' she said. 'How's it been here?'

'Great,' Dan said. 'We told everyone you had a breakdown. Couldn't take the pressure.' He grinned, but Beth wasn't convinced he was joking.

'Well, I'm fine now, so you can step aside, boys.'

Edie cheered her on and the atmosphere was good-natured. Beth was about to thank Oliver for the card but Edie called her over to say something important, then couldn't remember what. The boys left, and that was that.

A few days later Oliver said they were going down to the cafeteria, and she and Edie should come too, and they couldn't think of a good enough reason to turn him down, so they went.

Beth thought she'd never seen anyone sit as elegantly as Oliver, whose long legs folded over each other in perfect parallel lines. Despite the weather, his Oxford shirt was uncreased, his sandy hair stayed feathery and he smelled, as usual, of something that might have been expensive cologne or might just have been him. He looked clean. He smelled clean. Beth wondered if this were some innate talent of the white Anglo-Saxon Protestant male. Oliver appeared not to know how to sweat. His perfection impressed her.

'So, tell us all about the plague,' Oliver said. 'We heard that Edie snatched you from the jaws of death.'

'She did,' Beth said. 'The double jaws of death by flu and despair. For which I owe her my firstborn child.'

'Yeah.' Dan looked glum. 'My place is a slum too. Summer sublets are the pits.'

Oliver and Edie made sad noises.

'Look at them,' Dan said to Beth. 'Happily ensconced in desirable family real estate. Could they be any more smug?'

'We can't help it if we're locals,' Edie said, with her best sad face.

'They presume, don't you find,' Dan continued addressing Beth, 'that anyone who grew up in the city is superior to anyone who moves here? It's incredibly annoying.'

Beth considered this. 'But don't you think they're right? Everyone who grew up here seems vastly superior to me.'

'Case closed,' Edie said. 'Right, Ollie?'

Ollie? Beth looked at her friend.

'Obviously we value a bit of upstart energy,' Oliver said. 'Can't afford to let the gene pool stagnate.'

'Hands off my gene pool. I'm taking it back to Michigan,' Dan said. There was an edge to his voice.

Huh, thought Beth. She wondered what Oliver meant by 'upstart energy'. Generally unsullied by sophistication? Jewish?

They had barely finished eating when Edie stood up. 'Sorry, boys, but Beth and I have work to do. You'll have to have coffee without us.' And with that she took Beth's elbow and steered her out.

'Do we have work to do?'

'Not really,' Edie said. 'But I couldn't take much more of those two.'

'I thought they were nice.'

Edie scrunched up her face. 'Nice? Really?

Interesting take. You'll have to trust me on this one. We do not hang around with them except when we can't help it.'

So Beth was left once again to puzzle the parameters of 'their' attitude. *It was fun*, she wanted to say. *I like them*.

What did her instinct say? But if her instincts spoke at all, she couldn't hear them over the sound of Edie's voice.

14

Beth and Edie commuted together, ate lunch together and spent most of their spare time together – except Monday and Thursday evenings when Edie had her shrink, and Sunday mornings when she visited her grandmother. They laughed at each other's jokes. They laughed before they even got to the punchlines because they found each other's manner of telling jokes so hilarious. They sat in the park at lunchtime and rated couples on who was getting the worst deal, played 'Steal or Burn' about the clothes other women were wearing. They made up futures for people they'd never see again. Edie compulsively invented games, like 'Change One

Thing' that required them to improve people walking past.

'Lose ten pounds,' she'd say, or 'Ditch the shoes.'

'Everything,' Beth whispered to the mirror.

At work they split jobs, running relay so one or the other was in place before anyone even knew they needed help. They volunteered to work late, because you could go to only so many Happy Hours before officially becoming an alcoholic.

Unless there was a shooting or a traffic pile-up, their most frequent late-night companions were culture critics on first nights and obituary editors (a team of two recently increased to four), working long hours to keep up with the epidemic of AIDS deaths.

The obit team was assigned to what were irreverently called the 'Gay Sports Pages' – the record of dead young men, mainly in the arts. Every morning, readers across the city turned to the B-section first, curious and horrified to see which actors, artists, choreographers, dancers, directors, fashion designers and photographers had died. Newspaper policy meant that cause of death was never stated, but the age of the deceased did that. An orgy of youthful corpses.

Every straight woman in New York knew you could get caught in the AIDS crossfire by having sex with an addict, an ex-addict, a bisexual, or a not entirely straight man. Not to mention anyone who had ever had sex with any of the above. Men wore rubber-glove strength condoms, at least for the first few weeks of a relationship. Lesbians, it was said, used dental dams. It was a time of free love, high risk, easy death.

Dawn said that the guys who drank at Christopher Street bars – particularly the serious ones in leather and uniforms – hung out after dark at places like The Mineshaft, where things you couldn't even begin to imagine happened in anonymous back rooms.

'Like what?' Beth had asked, wondering at the limits of imagination.

'Like everything,' Dawn said. 'Glory holes. Crisco. Ten guys at once.'

Glory holes? Crisco? Ten guys at once doing what?

Edie said she'd started giving blood because if your donor card came back in the mail, you knew you weren't HIV-positive. It was more genteel than getting an AIDS test. Because who knew what that nice guy you met at a party had been up to before you? Not to mention the not-so-nice one.

Sex and death. The very air in New York City was heavy with it. Beth thought *Sex and Death* worked better as a motto than *So Good They Named it Twice*, or *I ❤ New York*. *Sex and Death*, or possibly *Sex, Death and Bagels*, which covered all bases, including food, which New Yorkers seemed to rank above sex and death in any case.

Beth chose bagels, or perhaps they chose her – in the absence of sex and death. The best bagels in town were sold every morning at the newspaper's cafeteria for twelve cents each. Everyone from editors to machinists to copy boys lined up for them, arriving still warm on huge metal trays from some kosher bakery in Brooklyn. They were smallish and pale gold, smooth and leathery outside and gloriously doughy within. At first, Beth bought extras to take home. But by the end of the day they'd unexpectedly turned to cement.

When a shocked Beth pulled two rock-hard bagels out of her bag and knocked them on the table, Edie grinned, delighted.

'All stale and petrified,' she cackled. 'Like our dreams, my friend. Like our dreams.'

On days they didn't work late, there was no shortage of establishments offering two-for-one giant frozen margaritas. Edie, Beth and the rest of young employed New York regularly got so drunk that the best they could do was to stagger to a taxi or fall into the subway and hope they didn't throw up at 72nd

Street. Once home, they passed out at eight and woke at midnight with a screaming hangover. Two screaming hangovers.

'Hell it was to be alive,' muttered Edie. 'But to be young was even worse.'

'Shhhhh,' whispered Beth, clutching her head and searching for painkillers.

After which they forsook Happy Hours for at least three days till they forgot the pain and could think of nothing nicer than gigantic goblets of sugar syrup, lime juice and triple sec heavily spiked with tequila. Two for the price of one. Bliss.

15

Beth found herself missing Tom. Or at least experienced irrational pangs that might have meant she missed him, while realising that such feelings were absurd. What did she miss after all? The confusing signals, the cul-de-sac conversations and awkward silences? The snide comments and endless bickering with Dawn? The refusal – or inability – to speak or act in a way that made any sense at all? He didn't even smile except at things he alone thought were funny. How could she miss someone so infuriating?

And yet, he slid into her mind.

Idiot, she told herself.

She decided to call the house, just to make sure

they'd found the cheque for her August rent. Not that they could have missed it, in an envelope on their bed with her explanatory note and new phone number. But she felt guilty about leaving so suddenly. Furtive. Or, at the very least, impolite.

She called from her desk late in the day, hoping Dawn might already be at work, but no one answered and she hung up. Annoyed. Mainly at herself.

Edie stuck her head around the corner. 'You ready to go?'

Beth nodded and Edie stepped into the cubicle, hands on hips. 'Why are you always frowning?'

'I am not frowning.'

'You are. Why don't you smile more?'

Beth made a face as they headed to the elevator.

'I'm serious,' Edie said. 'It's vital to smile. Every-one likes a person who smiles.'

'I'm sure you're correct, Pollyanna. Sadly, I have a terrible smile.'

'Don't be ridiculous.'

'I *do*. Look.' Beth smiled her lopsided, uncomfortable smile.

'Oh my God. You do!'

'See?'

'I see. I just never noticed. You'll have to practise smiling better.'

'Practise? Don't be stupid.'

'It's not stupid.' Edie was characteristically adamant. 'You can practise anything. Standing, walking, sitting in a chair, looking interested, flirting. What do you think they do all day at finishing school?'

'I've never once wondered what they do all day at finishing school.'

'Well, now you know.'

Beth shook her head. 'I'm not doing it.'

'You have to start somewhere. Remember my motto.'

'Excellent motto. Now go away.'

'I am going nowhere, my friend.'

And so, after supper and a gin and orange each,

Edie and Beth sat opposite each other at the table and locked eyes with tipsy intensity.

'Right,' Edie commanded. 'Go.'

Beth smiled. First a comedy smile, then a more serious one, a smile that made a genuine effort to be winning.

'It's tragically self-conscious. Plus, your eyes are anxious and you're slumping. You look shocking. Like a rockfish.'

'I told you.' Beth blinked. 'A what?'

'A rockfish. Terrible faces. Bug eyes. Turned-down mouths. You look just like one of them.'

'Great.'

'It's unfortunate, but as I always say, you have to start somewhere.'

'You do always say.'

'Let's do some exercises.' Edie hunched and relaxed her shoulders, opened her mouth as wide as possible, made circles with her arms.

Beth stared. 'I'm not doing that stuff.'

'Yes, you are. Start by sitting up straight, for God's sake. Relax your shoulders. Now think of something really nice. You don't have to tell me. We'll call it your magic moment.'

'I'm going to be sick.'

'Do as I say.'

Beth thought of her acceptance letter from the newspaper.

'Got something? OK. Think about it, hard, and look at me, and remember it and – now smile.'

She did.

'That's better. Now, slight three-quarter view, excellent. Magic moment. Three-quarter. Stand up straight or sit up straight if you're sitting. Simple.'

Beth did as she was told. They practised, rolling their heads around and singing in between to relax.

'Where'd you learn all this method idiocy?'

'I went on a Stella Adler summer course,' Edie said. 'It's what parents like mine make their kids do. For social enrichment.'

'Did you want to be an actress?'

'No. I just needed to avoid another summer hanging out at home. Anyway, stop distracting me.' She poured herself more gin. 'Now we go to Advanced Smiling. Advanced Smiling, for which you may or may not qualify, requires you to think of the other person, not yourself. Look at the other person, think of your moment, and then if they're attractive, think about them saying they want to have sex with you.'

'Bridge too far,' said Beth.

'Your lack of imagination defies belief.'

'It's not lack of imagination. It's lack of wanting to think about you wanting to have sex with me.'

'You don't think I'm attractive?'

Beth rolled her eyes. 'Also, I'm tired.'

'No, you're not. You're getting it. Try.'

Beth tried. She looked deep into Edie's eyes as she silently told her about the moment the envelope had arrived. 'We are pleased to inform you ...' For a moment she forgot herself.

'Excellent,' Edie said. 'It almost looked like you meant it for a second. Were you thinking of having sex with me?'

'No.'

'Your loss.'

Beth laughed. 'Can we stop?'

'We have to do it a thousand times before it sticks.'

'We don't have to do it a thousand times tonight. I've had a terrible smile my whole life, it could take decades to repair.'

'OK. But only because I've had too much to drink and need to lie down.'

Beth wondered what else she could improve. ('Stand up straight,' Edie nagged, more or less constantly. 'Women slouch to make themselves less threatening. It's pathetic. Shoulders back, head up. Like you're balancing a box of grenades.')

Grenades?

Beth thought a lot about sexual charisma. Why were some girls so popular when they weren't even good-looking? Edie had strong opinions on the subject.

'You can go a very long way if you believe you're amazing. You could argue it's delusional and fucked-up, but fucked-up people are more interesting anyway, don't you find?'

Beth blinked. She hadn't ever considered fucked-up people more interesting, but now she wondered if it was true.

Edie laughed. 'I like the way you never speak before thinking. It's a rare quality.'

'I like the way you never think before speaking,' Beth said. 'That's a rare quality too. And anyway, you say things that require thinking about. Most of the time I have no idea what to say.'

'Neither do I,' Edie said, 'but I always say something anyway, just in case of an awkward silence.' She shuddered. 'Nothing fills me with horror like an awkward silence.'

Beth looked at her friend. '*Nothing?* Genocide,

bubonic plague, fractures with the bones sticking out through the skin? Dentistry without anaesthetic? Tampon blood running down your legs in public? Snakebite?' She stopped to think. 'Gang rape? Really? Torture? *An awkward silence*? That's just …'

Edie shrugged. 'Now you see how twisted I am. Awkward silence versus genocide. No contest. It's wrong, clearly.'

'But …' Beth stared. 'You're not shallow or lacking compassion. If anything, it's the opposite. You're always thinking about other people.'

Edie sipped her gin. 'Maybe that's just a cloak to cover my lack of proper feelings.'

I wonder what constitutes proper feelings, Beth mused. It wasn't a concept she'd had cause to consider. Edie's feelings seemed OK to her. As a friend she was warm and funny and real. She drank too much, was a bit self-centred and possessive, but lots of people drank too much and Beth liked being possessed by Edie. Who wouldn't?

16

Edie taught Beth to be an amazing intern.

She taught her to make two coffees whenever she made herself one, to take the other into the department and ask if anyone else wanted it. Someone always did and was grateful.

Observing Edie's terror of an awkward silence taught Beth not to be scared of saying something, anything, to start up a conversation. You had to start somewhere, as Edie reminded her twenty times a day, and it turned out that people generally did want you to talk to them. If they weren't busy, they'd happily tell you about their job. Or how much they hated their boss. Or their boyfriend. If

119

they were busy, you left them alone. Unless they needed help.

Beth continued to practise her smile, and to do what Edie said she must, which was always to smile at everyone, even if they were horrible and told her to fuck off, which they sometimes did. But if you smiled, they usually felt guilty about it afterwards.

Edie taught her always to be the last one out of the department – out of the building if at all possible (not easy in a newspaper) – and to offer help to anyone, anytime, even if she didn't work for them.

She taught Beth not to apologise, except to say, 'I'm a complete idiot, I won't do that again,' because apologising just annoyed people and was more about how *you* felt.

The more she learned, the more Beth enjoyed the job. She loved knowing her way around the building. Most people knew how to do their own jobs, but she was learning what everyone else did too, and about the spaces between jobs. She knew when there was a weather story or a grisly murder that would keep whole departments at their desks till midnight, and what that meant for the lowest of the low, i.e. the interns, who got food in and helped with research when there was no one else to do it.

She loved being at the office late at night when the presses began to roll and the whole building vibrated. It made her feel she was working at the centre of the universe.

As the summer wore on, Jeanne juggled the interns, realigned them according to their strengths. Oliver and Edie made an entertaining pair, tall and short, with an excellent double act based on contrasting New York styles – WASP/Jew, preppy/artsy, reserved/noisy. They were fun to have around and particularly popular with less frantic departments like sales promotion. Dan and Beth had less charisma but worked extra hard to compensate.

Beth, however, found working with Dan problematic. It didn't help that he was four years older and always needed to be the best. He had his own agenda that did not involve sharing work, whereas Beth preferred collaboration. Dan barely spoke to her, made her feel unwelcome if she tagged along.

Jeanne watched her interns critically, and one evening called Beth into her office.

'Tell me about you and Dan,' she said without preamble.

Beth didn't know how to answer. 'He's OK,' she said.

'But?'

'Edie and I always shared the work. Dan just works on his own. Which is fine, I don't mind exactly …'

Jeanne sighed. 'Given a choice, I'd always prefer to hire girls,' she said. 'But as you've probably noticed, that's not how this place works.'

Unsure whether her opinion was being solicited, Beth waited. The silence grew as Jeanne tapped a pencil.

'OK,' she said at last. 'Do your best. I'll have a chat with Dan about collaboration. He does appear immune to the concept. Perhaps a drink after work, or lunch. Just the two of you. Worth a try?'

Beth nodded. 'I'll ask him,' she said. You had to start somewhere.

'Try softly-softly. If that fails, I'll break out the big guns.'

17

Though Edie still discouraged socialising outside work, on quiet days the four interns ate lunch together. Beth couldn't help her attraction to Oliver, whose sexual orientation wasn't really the point. His effortless poise took her breath away. She sometimes had a sense that Dan felt the same way about Oliver, but you could never really tell.

Edie said Dan suffered from Midwest syndrome, which was based on a (justifiable, according to her) sense of geographical inferiority. She explained this theory in detail as she and Beth drank frozen drinks after work.

'At least you're East Coast,' Edie said. 'Poor old

Dan probably comes from generations of dull Michigan factory workers, toiling away in Detroit on the Model T assembly line.'

Beth shook her head. 'Where on earth do you get your facts?'

'Facts?' Edie looked astonished. 'I make them up. But honestly, *Michigan*. I feel sorry for him. What has ever happened of any significance in Michigan aside from car factories?'

Beth considered. 'Motown?'

'Can Michigan truly claim Motown?'

'Uh, yes. I think you'll find that Detroit is located in the state of Michigan.'

'Fine. Answer me this. Does Dan look Black to you?'

Beth laughed. How could anyone argue with Edie? 'OK, you win. He's geographically disadvantaged, tragically un-Black and we should all feel sorry for him.'

'I wouldn't go that far,' Edie said. 'I don't feel sorry

for him. Nor do I want us to spend more time with him than is strictly necessary.' Her words to Beth were pointed. 'A policy you would do well to adopt.'

'Well, as a matter of fact that's working out fine,' Beth said. 'He's my partner for the next ten days but not working together is pretty much his modus operandi.'

'He's a rogue male, the Pale Rider of the intern fraternity.'

'He's just ambitious.'

'So are you. So am I. So was Stalin. We wouldn't have made it this far if we weren't. The difference is that you, Ollie and I have an all-for-one-and-one-for-all mentality. We are the Three Musketeers of Internville. While Dan is an every-man-for-himself, ruthlessly ambitious, throw-your-friends-under-a-bus kind of psychopath.'

'Like Stalin.'

'Exactly.'

'Don't exaggerate.'

'I never exaggerate.'

'You always exaggerate.'

Edie frowned. 'Only to prove a point.'

Beth suggested to Dan that they eat lunch together, but it wasn't a success. Dan kept looking at his watch, and at last got up to leave, claiming he had an order to pick up from the photo desk. Beth never really got a chance to broach the subject of working as a team.

Oliver and Edie arrived at her table just as Dan was leaving.

'How'd it go?' they asked, when the coast was clear.

'About as you'd expect,' Beth said. 'He left early to do some work I know nothing about.'

'Hmm,' said Oliver.

'Infuriating,' Edie said. 'Utterly tragic you have to work with him.'

'*Utterly tragic*,' Oliver said, with a perfect imitation of Edie's pout.

Edie hit him and laughed. Their easy intimacy caused Beth a stab of jealousy. Oliver had taken her place as Edie's partner and she was stuck working on her own. She looked forward to the next shuffle.

18

On Friday that week, the two girls planned a movie after work. Any movie would do, just for the popcorn and someone else's air conditioning, so they saw *Return of the Jedi* on a huge screen in Times Square. Arriving home, cheerful and giddy with starship battles and friend-love, the doorman tapped his nose and pointed a finger upwards.

'Your mother's here.'

Beth had observed disappointment in people's eyes. She'd seen shoulders sag, mouths turn down and faces fall. But never had she seen a person's entire bearing flip so abruptly from assurance to defeat.

Oh, she thought.

Edie was silent in the elevator. When the doors opened, her mother stood waiting for them. They didn't have time to arrange their faces.

'There you are,' she cried. 'I've been on the verge of calling the police!'

Edie's eyes narrowed. 'Really? To say what? Your daughter was supposed to be home from work a few hours ago, but she might have gone out for a drink or dinner or even, possibly, worked late? And by the way she had no idea I was coming, so wouldn't have mentioned her plans. The police would be very impressed with that story. Especially once you told them I was nineteen.'

'Oh, no need for sarcasm, Edie. Why don't you introduce me to your friend.' She raised an eyebrow. 'So, you're Beth. The lucky roommate.'

'Lucky?' Edie spat the word. 'I *asked her* to come live here. To keep me company.'

Beth had to think hard to remember when she'd felt so belittled. Edie's mother's face wore a smile that said, *I do hope you appreciate how generous we've been, offering you a free place to stay.* Unless she was imagining it. Which she wasn't.

She glanced at Edie, who had pulled the shutters down and left town.

Beth had never observed such a psychologically loaded operative. Mothers and daughters, of course, there was often an edge, and many of her friends had messy home lives – but this! Her own humiliation made her act as you might to save a drowning kitten.

She forced a smile. 'Such a shame we didn't know you were coming, Mrs Gale,' she said. 'It's our weekend for overtime and we both have to work.'

'Overtime? How absurd. You're interns. No one expects an intern to work weekends. Edie will call and explain. Won't you, darling?'

Edie rose to the occasion with her best sad look. 'It doesn't work that way. I mean, if we'd had some notice maybe we could have swapped.'

'It's not too late to swap. Just call and tell them …'

Beth and Edie both looked at the clock. It was after eleven.

'If only we'd had time to plan,' Beth said.

'I know.' Edie shook her head sorrowfully.

Edie's mother stood by in helpless fury.

'I'm going to bed.' Edie stood up and left the room.

'We have to be up early. Really nice to meet you, Mrs Gale, and thank you for letting me stay.'

Mrs Gale sputtered. 'I can't believe—'

Beth fled.

The following morning, Edie knocked lightly on Beth's door at eight thirty. She was already dressed and the girls slipped out minutes later. When the elevator doors shut, Edie slumped.

'Oh, thank God. Have you ever seen anything like her?'

Beth was silent for a moment. 'She's something, all right.'

'Something from your worst nightmare.'

Beth had never seen anything like her. Nor had she seen anything like Edie's reaction to her. Catastrophic deflation. It was like watching the *Hindenburg* burn.

'A whole day to fill.' Edie wore gloom like a cloak. 'What on earth will we do?'

'We'll think of something.'

They headed downtown till they found a dark coffee shop, unlikely to be entered by anyone they knew or would want to know. Feeling like spies in East Berlin, they took a booth all the way at the back and only then relaxed.

'She won't follow us here.' Edie stared at the door.

Beth blinked. 'Of course she won't, idiot. She's not the Gestapo.'

Edie didn't laugh. 'No? I'd say wanting to control every single aspect of my life is pretty scary. Isn't it? I haven't ever had any other mother so how would I know? I guess yours isn't like her?'

'Oh my God, Edie. No one's like her.' Beth thought

of her own mother. The periods of depression, the locked past.

Edie went on. 'I do meet other mothers now and then, and they all seem pretty harmless. How did I end up the lucky one?'

'I can see why you're in therapy. But surely she's the one who needs help.'

'Not according to her. She says the purpose of her shrink is to help her deal with me. And my dad goes along with whatever she says. Some people shouldn't be allowed to have kids.'

Edie looked so gloomy that Beth felt a rush of sympathy. 'You need to move somewhere,' she said. 'Somewhere really far. I mean, I know it's extreme and normally I don't advocate running away, but I don't think you have much choice. Somewhere like Tonga.'

'Where's Tonga?'

'I don't know. Middle of the Pacific.'

Edie sighed. 'I'm so glad to have you as a witness. A lot of people are taken in by her. I mean, she can seem charming if you have no insight at all into the human psyche. I'm always amazed when people tell me they think she's nice. You knew immediately, didn't you? It's not me. She's not *nice*.'

'It's not you. She's definitely not nice. I was ready to kill myself before she even knew my name. I mean, it's kind of a skill if you think of it that way. An evil soul-sucking skill.' Beth's lightness of tone belied the desperation she felt for her friend. 'Doesn't your therapist help?'

'I've been going for six years and it doesn't seem to have solved anything. I haven't killed myself yet, so I guess that's something.'

Beth felt a jolt of fear. 'Don't kill yourself, please, Edie. I'd cry.'

A pale smile. 'Thank you. That's nice.'

'It's true. I'm ordering breakfast.'

She ordered half a cantaloupe with cottage cheese, and coffee. Edie ordered the same.

'What can we do today? It's too hot to walk and

too hot to go to the park. Too hot to do anything outdoors.'

Edie sipped coffee and sighed. 'We could go to work.'

'I'm not that desperate. What's the nearest museum?'

'The Met. Eighty-first and Fifth.'

'I've never been.'

'What? Never? How is that even possible?'

'When would I go to the Met? This is my first time in New York and in case you hadn't noticed, we spend all our time working and drinking.'

'God, you've led a sheltered life. We'll walk through the park. Shuffle slowly in the shade. Sit on a bench when we start to melt.'

Beth chanted it. 'Shuffle-slowly-in-the-shade. Sit-on-a-bench-when-we-start to-melt.'

She grinned at Edie, who turned away.

19

After breakfast, they headed across Central Park, walking slowly to the rhythm of Beth's new mantra, hugging the shade. The Met had just opened, they paid a voluntary dollar each, then wandered around and chose the best-looking man in every painting until it was nearly lunchtime. Beth loved how easy it was to appreciate art in the company of someone who shared your sense of humour. Afterwards, they split a piece of cake in the café.

'Is it always this hot here?'

'Most summers. That's why everyone goes to the Hamptons.'

Beth finished off the cake and scraped the plate. 'Why'd your mother come back without telling you?'

'To check up on me.'

'To check what, exactly? It's not like you're twelve.'

'That I haven't "harmed" myself.' Edie laughed a sad laugh. 'Become a coke addict. Or ruined her chairs. Ironically, the thing that makes me want to kill myself most is her.'

Beth was out of her depth with this version of Edie. She wanted to ask if she really thought about killing herself but didn't dare, in case it was true. Her own family story stressed survival. Kristallnacht and forged visas, travel across borders at night, days in hiding, weeks in waiting, the loss of everything except hope. Twelve members of her mother's family had died in Auschwitz. Her father's family had been decimated; his youngest sister alone emerged, reset-tled in Amsterdam, and slit her wrists after the birth of her first child. Most of this information she had

138

gleaned from overheard conversations. Her parents rarely spoke of loss. Beth often wondered if they spoke to each other on the subject. She sometimes felt as if she had inherited the gross accumulation of her parents' silence, the weight of an immeasurable, unacknowledged horror planted within her like the seed of some hungry vine.

They left the Met and found shade under a tree in Central Park. The beat of New York filtered through from every direction.

Surviving summer, Beth thought, required moving as little as possible. Motionless, you could achieve a Zen state in which your outline softened and you mutated into a shimmering pool of energy. Lying on her back, she stared at the branches overhead.

'You're not seriously going out with Mike again, are you?' Mike was the guy on the city desk.

Edie didn't answer immediately. 'I'm not going out with him seriously, if that's what you mean.'

'That's not what I mean.'

'Can't I at least see what he's like?'

'You know what he's like. He's like a man with a pregnant wife dating an intern half his age.'

'You shouldn't oversimplify moral situations. Maybe he's not happy.'

'Maybe he's a creep.'

'Stop being so fucking principled.'

'If you were as boring as I am, you'd find it easy.'

Edie laughed. 'You just wait. Someday you'll find yourself shoving old ladies and babies out of your way on to the last lifeboat of the *Titanic* and then you'll think, "My friend Edie told me many years ago that moral choices could be ugly as hell."'

'I'll call you when I crack so you can say I told you so. Are there plans to get the *Titanic* up and running again?'

'Don't be so literal.'

The sun started inching its way up their legs. 'Ugh,' Beth said. 'I'm so comfortable. Do we have to move?'

'We should have brought an umbrella.'

'We should have brought a beach.'

Edie sighed. 'We're going to have to do this tomorrow too, you know.'

'That'll be hell. Think of the positives. Your mother has turned into the perfect catalyst for getting us out into the world. It's what parents are supposed to do, nudge their fledglings off the perch.'

Edie put on a radio announcer voice. 'Fledgling One is flapping, flapping, flapping! Plummeting! Crashing! Oh, the humanity!' But she wasn't smiling.

'I don't suppose she has any good qualities?'

Edie focused on the middle distance. 'I can't tell anymore. It's like we were shouting at each other when the wind changed and now we're stuck like this forever. My shrink says I should try to reconnect with the mother I loved as a child, but I have no memory of that person. Either of them. Her or me.'

Beth thought about this. 'Why do you think she's so awful?'

'I don't know. I suppose her mother was awful too. Away all the time having a successful career. How dare she, right? I really love my grandma, but I'm not convinced she was much of a mother. Which she passed on to her daughter, who's a lousy mother, and I guess if I ever had kids, I'd be a lousy mother too. It's a pretty depressing legacy, don't you think?'

'What makes you think you'd be like your mother? Isn't the fact that you're already worried about being a bad mother proof that you won't be?'

'My shrink says that. But I don't see how it follows. I'm thinking of leaving Dr Lieb anyway. Six years is long enough. And anyway, why wouldn't I make the same mistakes? And anyway *anyway*, I no longer care. There's no way I'm ever having kids.'

'Really?' Beth had always assumed she'd have kids. Not that she particularly wanted them, it was just what you did.

'Yes. Really. Never.' She propped herself up on one elbow and looked at Beth. 'You're a good friend. You ask all the right questions. And I like hanging out with you. But you kind of have to accept that there's no fix here. It's just ugly. Sex is one of the few things that makes me forget about myself for a while.'

Beth couldn't say, *I know exactly what you mean*, because she didn't.

20

Edie and Beth floated around New York City as if it were the Dead Sea, propelling themselves slowly through the murky air with a combined effort of arms and legs. They drifted out the bottom of the park, down through Times Square, across the garment district to Tenth Avenue and Chelsea, Edie telling Beth she hadn't lived till she'd eaten at the Empire Diner.

With a few blocks still to go, Edie stopped.

She looked up. 'Wait! I know someone who lives here. I went to school with him.' They crossed the street, and Edie searched the buzzers. 'Hello? Leo? It's Edie! We're standing outside your building! Can we come in?'

Beth couldn't hear what he answered but the front door buzzed and Edie pushed it open to a filthy lobby. 'You'll love Leo, he's the coolest.'

Leo was the coolest. He lived in a studio, a small room with a bathroom in what might once have been a closet, and a hot plate and mini-fridge instead of a kitchen. The place was filled with records and books stacked high in blue plastic milk crates or balanced on shelves made of planks and bricks. Concert posters – not the ones you buy, the ones you steal off the wall at a gig – covered the walls. A rusty old fan spun noisily in the centre of the room, ruffling papers, the covers of music magazines and some of the insufficiently Blu-tacked posters. A single mattress in the corner had nothing on it but a sheet, a crumpled pillow and an ashtray. Even that seemed cool.

Leo's room smelled strongly of grass, cigarettes and sweat. Some hippieish incense burned in a corner to add to the mix – or maybe to cover up the smell of everything else. Under everything was the all-pervasive smell of raw, unwashed Leo.

'Hey,' he said when Edie introduced Beth. And then to Edie, 'Long time no see. How you been?' He spoke with the distinct inflection of an urban Black kid, despite being white and a graduate of Edie's fancy private school.

Edie told him about their summer job, and her mother's appearance from the Hamptons, and how they were out on the town avoiding her. Leo nodded, with the air of finding Edie's bourgeois Upper West Side problems faintly amusing. The fan was noisy, and when it started to clatter, he turned it off for a few seconds and back on again.

'I think I got just the thing for your troubles, Edie my friend.' He looked at Beth. 'And your problems too, Edie's friend.'

With that, he dug under the mattress and pulled out a brown envelope, from which he removed a baggie full of white powder, tapped a small heap out on to the back of a Velvet Underground album, cut it into lines and handed Edie a rolled-up ten-dollar bill.

'Fifty bucks worth of happy. My treat.'

Beth watched as Leo went next, snorting up three lines to Edie's two, then held the tube out to her. She hesitated for a second and then took it, hoping her hand didn't shake.

It wasn't hard to imitate, and she did, feeling the numbing effects of cocaine at the back of her throat and tongue, a slightly unpleasant sensation, offset by the whoosh of a soaring elation in her brain. *Oh my God*, she thought. *This is fantastic. Why didn't anyone tell me? Or maybe they did and I didn't believe them.* Edie and Leo were talking about going for a walk, and then they were out the door, down the stairs and on to the street where, walking along the sidewalk behind them, Beth felt she was on one of those moving airport travelators so that each step carried her further than it should and her feet seemed to propel her along much faster and smoother than her usual walking pace and she was sure she could keep up this uncannily smooth and steady glide more or less forever which made her laugh and wonder why walking didn't always feel this amazing so much more mind-blowing for instance than taking a bus and look they were already at the Empire Diner and going in to have breakfast even though it was afternoon and anyway hadn't she and Edie eaten breakfast just a few hours ago? All the pictures on the menu looked so delicious she didn't know what to order not being hungry and yet wanting to taste everything she saw on other people's plates. *Waffles*, she thought, *when did I last eat a waffle, and why haven't I had more waffles in my life because waffles are so delicious though the word itself is kind of strange, waffle waffle waffle, woff-ell. Off-ell. Awful.* Why had she never noticed before that *awful* and *waffle* were practically the same word, what a weird coincidence.

Leo and Edie ordered the all-day breakfast pan-cakes. She ordered waffles and tried explaining her revelation to them but they didn't seem as interested as she thought they'd be. The delicious elation began to fade.

Come back, she thought. *Come back, beautiful feeling!*

When they arrived, her waffles disappointed her greatly because she wasn't hungry and mainly wanted to lie down and go to sleep.

What happened to the colours?

God, she felt low.

The prospect of seeing Edie's mother again made her want to cry.

Maybe she'd have to move back to her slum in the Village. The slum in the Village also made her want to cry.

They returned to Leo's apartment where Leo rolled a joint and shared it with Edie, but Beth shook her head when he passed it, feeling weird enough already, low and a little sick. Leo put the Velvet Underground album on the turntable and Edie lay on his bed, eyes closed, while Nico sang 'I'll Be Your Mirror' in her breathy German accent. Beth wanted to leave but didn't know if Edie was asleep or just too stoned to move, so she sat on the floor, leafing through some of Leo's music magazines. He half hummed, half sang along with the music as if unaware she was still there.

Beth had experienced enough awkward situations in her life to not particularly mind this one. She would just flip pages and think about other things till it was time to go.

Across the room Leo rolled another joint, came and sat down on the floor next to her and offered it again.

'No thanks,' she said.

'Hey, babe, what's wrong?'

'Nothing's wrong,' Beth said, thinking, *Don't call me babe*. 'I've just had enough. Thanks.'

Leo inhaled deeply, then turned to Beth, grabbed her head in both hands and kissed her, exhaling smoke into her mouth. She pushed him away, coughing.

'I said no thanks.' But she said it politely, not with any resentment or anger. She didn't know how to address the matter of him kissing her when there was clearly nothing between them, not even a flirtatious glance, not wanting to offend him as he was Edie's friend. He was staring at her now, and moved closer, trapping her against the wall so she couldn't move away without a struggle. And then he had his hands up her shirt and under her bra, and his tongue in her mouth, and he was leaning his weight on her so she felt panicky and trapped but still didn't want to make a loud noise and wake Edie, who might laugh or condemn her for not treating their host nicely, after he gave them all that coke for free.

She struggled but he was strong and incredibly

insistent, pinning her with one knee and holding both her wrists in one of his hands while unzipping his jeans.

'Come on, babe,' he murmured. 'It's just a little fun.'

But then he was on his knees pushing her head towards his erect penis until she could feel the solid fleshy tip pressing hard against her mouth and she twisted free and shouted, 'Get off me!'

Edie blinked and opened her eyes and sat up slowly. Leo shoved Beth and turned away to zip himself up so by the time Edie noticed what was going on, there was nothing going on.

'Hey, Leo,' Edie said. 'This is some great shit you got. What's up, Beth?'

Beth was on her feet now. 'Let's go,' she said.

Edie frowned. 'But Leo has more coke, don't you, Leo? The party's only getting started.'

Leo had his back to them.

Beth approached Edie and grabbed her arm, hard.

'I want to go.' And when Edie started to protest, she said, '*Now.*'

'OK, OK. Hold your horses, I gotta find my shoes. Hey, Leo, where's my shoes? My little friend here isn't cool with our big city ways. I think she's having a bad trip. Better take her home.'

She found her shoes and put them on, while Beth stood with the door to the apartment open, ready to bolt. Leo had his headphones on and his eyes closed. His body language made it clear he was done with them.

Out in the hall at last, Edie closed the apartment door behind her and turned to Beth. 'What was all that about? You see a ghost or something?'

'Your friend tried to ...' she started, unable to go on. She was trembling.

'Hey, no no no! Leo isn't like that,' Edie said. 'You probably misinterpreted what he said.'

'What he *did.*' But she wasn't about to describe it for Edie's benefit. And anyway, Edie was stoned.

'I guess you have to know Leo to appreciate him. He's kind of an oddball, but we've been friends since, like, forever. He always gets the best stuff and he's so generous. Perfect friend.'

Beth set her jaw, thinking, *Perfect asshole*. Getting to know him was not on the cards. She felt disgusted that he'd touched her, furious at herself for hesitating to offend him. *Asshole*.

When they arrived home, Beth shut herself in her room, certain they stank of dope so Edie's mother would immediately understand that they hadn't been at work. Emerging from the shower, she could hear a vicious fight taking place between mother and daughter.

'When are you ever going to grow up and be responsible?'

'Responsible? Don't make me laugh. You don't know the meaning of the word!'

'And you don't think of anyone but yourself. It didn't occur to you I'd have dinner waiting?'

'*I was working.*'

'Till nine o'clock?'

'It's a newspaper! People work twenty-four hours!'

'People like *you*? Don't make me laugh. And besides, you've been smoking marijuana. Do you do that at work?'

'How do you even know what it smells like?'

'Do I look stupid to you?'

'What do you think?'

'Don't you dare –'

'Oh, fuck you!'

'– use that language with me!'

'Fuck *fuck fuck fuck* FUCK.'

Beth pressed a pillow over her ears until the slam of a door indicated the end of the argument. She lay in bed thinking about cocaine and the awful cold insistence of Leo and his horrible erection. She thought about herself, how even when he was forcing himself on her, she was mostly worried about waking Edie, as if being polite were somehow more important than – whatever.

Get out of my head.

It was too early to sleep and she hated thinking of Edie and her mother just beyond the bedroom wall. The roar of the air conditioners, usually so soothing, made her brain itch. *I have to get out of here*, she thought.

Listening for silence, she took her key and cracked open the bedroom door. All clear. She slipped out. The bright empty corridor and white light of the elevator felt eerie. The doorman didn't acknowledge her. Outside, the air temperature was the same as her blood.

Taxis sped past. Over on Broadway, the Korean grocer blazed with light. Walking calmed her.

She checked her watch: not yet ten.

Passing a phone booth, she dug in her pocket for a dime and dialled her old number. Dawn would be at work. The phone rang eight times.

'What?'

'Tom. Hi.' He was silent. 'It's Beth.'

'I know.' He paused. 'Why are you calling?'

'No reason.'

'Did something happen? Been thrown out of your new place?'

'No,' she said. 'Nothing's happened.'

'Huh.'

'How's the Village?'

'How do you think?'

Hot, stinking, noisy. 'Scavenge anything good lately?' She felt desperate to keep him talking.

His voice brightened. 'Found an entire *Encyclopaedia Britannica* in its original bookcase. Nineteen fifty-five. Pretty cool. Couple of bamboo chairs. Framed print of Turin.'

'Turin?'

'Yeah, but it's nice. And a set of old army blankets.'

'What'll you do with those?'

'They're thick. Give 'em out to bums I guess.'

'In this weather?'

'They've got to be more comfortable to lie on than the sidewalk.'

What an odd person he was. 'Nothing else?'

'What were you expecting?'

'Right,' she said, noticing how often he answered a question with another question. 'I'd better go.'

She could hear him breathing.

'Tom?'

'Mmm?'

'Hang up.'

He clicked off.

Back home, she opened the apartment door silently and crept into bed. *His voice in the night*, she thought as she fell asleep. *Strangely reassuring.*

The following morning she woke up feeling awful.

'I'm taking the jitney back to the Hamptons this morning,' Edie's mother told them, frostily. 'So don't

158

bother rushing home from "work".' She bracketed the word with her fingers.

'We won't,' Edie said.

And then in a quick turnaround voice, her mother said, pleading, 'I do worry about you, sweetheart. Beth, keep an eye on my little girl, won't you please?'

Beth felt sick. She and Edie left the house without saying goodbye, confirming Edie's treachery as a daughter and Beth's blatant unsuitability as a friend.

That they were, in fact, lying to Edie's mother about going to work, and thus as blatantly dishonest as their accuser believed, never really occurred to either of them.

21

Depression settled on Beth and Edie like dust. It was too hot to walk the streets, so they returned to yesterday's breakfast place and ordered coffee, because, as Edie observed, they didn't serve hemlock.

'Will you come see my grandma with me? You'll love her. She's my only sane relative.'

She wanted to tell Edie what had happened with Leo yesterday but didn't know how to raise the subject. She had a feeling Edie wouldn't welcome hearing about it. Or would figure out a way to blame her. She pushed Leo out of her brain, but a wave of revulsion rose whenever he surfaced.

'She lives in a building full of artists. Terrible neighbourhood. But the place is amazing. You'll see.'

They headed west from the subway along increasingly grim blocks lined with crumbling buildings and abandoned cars. Vagrants shouted to themselves. Rent boys in make-up and crop tops wheedled for money. Under the derelict West Side Highway, shady commerce thrived: drugs, stolen cars, 'used' audio equipment. Half-dressed women tottered on high heels, most too old or too young for the work. An old tramp dressed in layers and layers of colourless rags pissed in a dribbling arc against the side of a building.

They reached the entrance, pushed through into the lobby and Edie greeted the man at the desk.

'Hi, Frank.'

'You're a good girl, Edie, visiting your grandma all the time.' He waved them through to the elevators.

Edie giggled as the doors closed. 'He says exactly

the same thing every time I come. Like it's the only sentence he knows in English.'

They knocked on Edie's grandmother's door, which was opened by an old woman with perfect posture, white hair and bright red lipstick.

'Edie!'

'Grandma!' Edie said and hugged her with the enthusiasm of a small child. 'This is Beth, Grandma. Beth, this is the infamous Clara Danzig.'

'Nonsense. Come in, come in. It's no day to be out on the streets. Come in where it's cool!'

Inside the apartment, fans blew in criss-cross paths through the large, high-ceilinged single room; four immensely tall windows flanked by high metal bookcases faced the shady side of the courtyard.

'I've made iced coffee. Sit, sit.' Edie leaped up to take the tray from her grandmother, who protested that she wasn't entirely infirm yet.

Beth, meanwhile, gazed from one gilded tableau to the next: an antique brocade sofa stacked with embroidered cushions, a mirrored coffee table covered in photography books and heavy strings of amber beads. A beautiful gold and green Japanese triptych above the sofa. Stained-glass panels leaning on window sills and fine old Oriental rugs on woodblock floors. Framed photographs interspersed with painted landscapes in ornate frames, old portraits, woodcuts and Indian reverse-glass paintings. The corner of the studio that Clara Danzig used as a bedroom held a carved Indian daybed draped in layers of paisley wool shawls. It looked like something out of the *Arabian Nights*.

Clara smiled. 'I collected things on my travels,' she said. 'Too many things. But the places I reported from hadn't yet been stripped by tourists.' She squinted at Edie. 'How are you, my dear? You look peaky.'

Edie smiled. 'No, Grandma. Just the usual.'

The old woman tutted. 'I feel responsible, but then, my mother was impossible too. It skips a generation in this family, or at least that's what Edie and I tell each other.' She winked at Edie and turned to look at Beth. 'You're not from Manhattan?'

Beth shook her head. It depressed her that this fact was so immediately obvious to everyone.

But Clara nodded approval. 'That's good. New Yorkers are too excitable. Frenzy without meaning, no time to think.'

'*It's bad for the soul.*' Edie parroted her grandma's voice.

Clara nodded. 'That's right. You girls need to look after your souls. No one else will do that for you.' She turned to Edie, pulled her close and kissed the top of her head. 'My darling. Life will get easier.' And chuckled. 'Then harder, then easier again.'

Edie pulled out books of photographs and Clara told stories of the places she'd visited, all of which Edie seemed to know by heart.

After an hour, Clara looked at her watch. 'I must get dressed. I'm having lunch upstairs with the boys.'

The boys, Edie explained, were the puppet-maker and theatre-director couple who'd moved to New York from Cameroon. 'The three of them are the building's worst clique,' she said, nodding at her grandmother.

'I'm photographing their retrospective,' said Clara, smiling. 'Though no one's commissioned it yet.' She went to the carved wardrobe and pulled out a long Japanese kimono, refreshed her lipstick, chose an old-fashioned Rolleiflex from the four cameras above her bed and loaded it. 'Move over here,' she said to the girls, pointing to the yellow sofa. 'Now sit closer.'

They sat together with their arms around each other smiling and Beth didn't have time to do her best non-awkward smile for the camera.

'Not cheese, please God,' Clara muttered, looking down into the camera. She snapped a single shot and the girls collapsed apart. 'Now serious, please. Sit up. I want profiles. Look in opposite directions.'

They complied. As the shutter clicked, Beth had a strange feeling about the photo, like a hint of future déjà vu.

'Good,' said Clara. In the hall, she hugged Edie and shook hands gravely with Beth, saying she'd walk up a floor while the girls took the elevator. 'Take care of Edie,' she said to Beth, who felt a now-familiar flicker of annoyance. Edie's entire family treated her as an unpaid custodian. 'And yourself,' Clara added.

'Wow,' Beth said when the elevator doors had closed.

'I told you.'

'And that apartment! I feel as if I've been to Timbuktu. Hail me a litter pulled by matching snow leopards!'

Edie had cheered up. 'Any good genes in the family come from her,' she said. 'She may have been a tricky mother but she's a lovely grandma.'

'How does your mother feel about you seeing her?'

'Strictly speaking,' Edie said, 'she doesn't know. She'd steal that from me too.'

'Don't you think you're a little paranoid?'

'Am I?'

'I hope you are, anyway.' Beth paused. 'Does your mother see her?'

'Rarely. They don't get along. My mother thinks she's an irresponsible show-off and doesn't forgive her for ten thousand abuses in the past.'

'Did she have a husband?'

'He died fifteen years ago. Another journalist, like virtually everyone they knew. All dipsomaniacs who smoked a thousand cigarettes a day. I don't remember him.' Her backstory flared with scraps of exotic history.

Beth looked at her watch. 'What shall we do now?'

'Let's go home. She'll be gone, and I could use a rest. It's all been way too emotional.'

22

'Coast clear,' said the doorman with professional deadpan.

Despite the hour, Edie and Beth found half a bottle of vodka, mixed it with orange juice, and finished it off with the sense of having vanquished something together, like two St Margarets, each with a foot on the neck of a dragon.

Edie checked the answerphone. 'What's this?' she said and played it again.

'*You alive?*' Two words, that was it.

Beth recognised the voice and was glad. She looked at Edie and shrugged.

The vodka worked its magic and they began to

cheer up. Then with a clink of her glass on Beth's, Edie said, 'So, who would you rather sleep with, Dan or Oliver?'

Beth's eyes shot open. 'Oh my God, *what*? Neither!'

'You have to choose.'

'I am not choosing. Why do I have to?'

'It's the game.' Edie glared at her.

'Then you go.'

'Fine.' Edie had clearly given it a good deal of thought. 'They're both impossible, obviously. Oliver already looks like his dad, or someone's dad anyway, no idea if his dad is gay too, but you know what I mean, that eternal preppy middle-aged thing. Anyway, you pretty much know what you're going to get there. From behind, no kissing.'

Beth covered her face with her hands. 'No! Stop!'

'Whereas Dan's so competitive, he'd probably race you to see who'd come first.'

'*Edie!!*'

'On the other hand, he'd definitely be worried you'd be scoring him against other boyfriends, so he'd make a serious effort in the sex department.'

Beth nearly choked on her drink. 'The *sex* department? *The sex department? What sex department?* Oh my God, does every office have one? Hello, reception, give me The Sex Department. I hear there's an opening in the …' But she couldn't finish.

'For a nice girl you have a terrible mind. Look at you. What would Louisa May Alcott say?'

'Beth dies, so you better be nice to me.'

'Never read it, never will.'

'Ignorance is nothing to be proud of. And I feel certain your mother would agree.'

Edie shook her head. 'Don't even joke about my mother. As far as I'm concerned, there's no humour in the subject.'

'Fine. So, you're saying Dan? Because he's competitive – not to *mention* heterosexual – he'd be better in The Sex Department?'

'That's my logic. Plus, gay Oliver wears white Y-fronts, you mark my words, and you probably don't want to have sex with a gay man in New York at this exact moment in time. AIDS, et cetera.'

'*AIDS, et cetera?* Oh, please, please stop, Edie. How am I ever going to look at either of them again? Or you for that matter.'

'Well, I don't see why you should bother.' Edie huffed. 'They're both exceedingly sub-standard.'

'Then why do we have to have sex with them?'

Edie shook her head, despairing. 'Don't you ever play subway sex? What in actual fact is wrong with you?' Edie's eyes were large and somewhat crossed. 'I do it all the time. It's just an extension of the game kids play – if you had to eat a spider or a cockroach, be blind or have no arms.'

'What kids did you hang out with?'

'You definitely played those games. Everyone did.'

Beth shook her head. 'Cross my heart. Although

now you mention it, we did play spy games involving bondage.'

'Wholesome suburban S and M.'

'Meanwhile, back in *The Sex Department*, they're working flat out.'

Edie laughed and poured the dregs of the vodka into her glass. 'We gotta find another bottle.' She crawled on all fours to the liquor cabinet and pulled long-forgotten bottles out of the dim recesses. 'Cherry eau de vie? What even is that? Cointreau? Pernod? Right. We're going on a bear hunt.'

'A bear hunt?'

'For vodka. We have to pretend to be sober, they don't like selling to inebriated ladies. Or gendle-hams.' Edie giggled.

'Gendlehams? Maybe I should do the talking.'

'I've got the ID.'

'I've got the ID too.'

'Mine's real. I'll go in. The guy who works there is cute.' She swayed a little.

They walked down the block arm in arm, as much for support as affection, and Beth waited outside while Edie went in for vodka. It felt like a very long time before she came out, with a brown paper bag out of which stuck a bottle of cheap vodka. She looked triumphant.

'He's coming over later.'

Beth blinked. 'What?'

Edie shushed her. 'The cute guy! He gets off work at five.'

'Are you serious?'

'He's really nice. You'll like him.'

'What if he's an axe murderer?'

'Liquor store guy? He's not an axe murderer. He's way too cute.'

'What if he's a *cute* axe murderer?'

Edie laughed. 'He's *not* an axe murderer, you'll see.' She stumbled.

Beth didn't want to see. For more reasons than could be listed on the back of a paper bag, she didn't want a complete stranger coming up to get drunk(er) with them on a Sunday evening. The invitation struck her as compromising verging on dangerous, and she dreaded both the intrusion and the responsibility for making sure her friend was safe. Was it her responsibility? She didn't much like the idea of finding Edie in a pool of blood in the morning and having to explain to her psycho parents what happened.

'Do you even know his name?'

'Nick. Ha. Fooled you.'

'So that's all fine then.'

'You're mad at me.' Edie tried to nuzzle her neck as they walked along.

'Don't be ridiculous. I'm not mad.' She was mad.

'You are. Don't be. It'll be fun, you'll see!'

When they got up to the apartment, Edie poured herself a large glass of vodka and added a single ice cube. Beth siphoned off half into her own glass and added orange juice to both.

'Hey!' Edie said, reaching for the bottle.

'A toast – to vodka.' Beth held her glass out to clink, but really she'd had enough. Her friend was smashed, getting more smashed and cute liquor-store guy would be arriving soon. Beth looked in the fridge for something to absorb the alcohol.

She found a loaf of bread and pulled it out. 'You want a sandwich? Or toast?'

Edie refilled her glass. 'No thanks. You have some. I'm getting dressed for my date. Wanna help me choose what to wear?' But she left without waiting for an answer.

Beth toasted the bread, added butter, picked up the plate and went to her room. She stuffed the toast in her mouth, starving suddenly, and halfway through her desultory meal, realised she felt wretched. The word rose in her gorge; she made it to the bathroom and retched. Sitting on the floor for a long time she leaned against the tiled wall, headachy and depressed. A trickle between her legs made her groan, and she hauled herself upright, grabbed a tampon and threw her bloody underwear in the sink. *Perfect*, she thought. With a feeling that she probably stank, she had a shower, rubbed the soap over the crotch of her underpants, brushed her teeth, drank a full glass of water with a couple of aspirin and passed out in bed.

If Nick from the liquor store ever did arrive, she didn't see or hear him. She woke at 1 a.m. with a hangover, but the apartment was silent, and eventually she dozed off again.

In the morning there was no sign of him, and on the way to work she and Edie hid behind a veil of don't-even-speak-my-head-hurts-too-much.

23

Dan had his head down researching a story for the magazine and Edie disappeared upstairs to see Mike, so Beth and Oliver went together to the cafeteria.

'Good weekend?' he asked.

'Yeah, great.' She didn't meet his eyes.

He frowned. 'Bad weekend?'

She didn't answer.

'Sorry I asked.'

Beth sighed. 'It was fine. Aside from being molested by Edie's friend from school. After a few lines of coke and a joint. And getting in the middle of World War Three between Edie and her crazy mother.'

'Wow. That sounds …' He hesitated.

'Horrible? It was.'

Oliver was not on comfortable ground. 'Who was the guy?'

'Sleazy rich boy. Lives in a dump. Lots of drugs. Kept calling me "babe".'

Oliver grimaced. 'Bet he's a dealer.'

'Maybe,' Beth said. 'I guess that's how he affords his glamorous lifestyle.'

'Where was Edie during the … incident?'

'She was in a drugged stupor across the room. And then when I made her leave, she told me I was making a big fuss over nothing.' Beth shook her head. 'It was awful. Sometimes I think New Yorkers are all just soulless zombies.'

'Except you, Oliver,' said Oliver.

'Except you, Oliver. You're definitely not a soulless zombie. But … so many people on the make here. And I'm such an outsider.'

'Anyone who lives in New York is a New Yorker.'

'It's different,' she said. 'You natives all seem impervious to doubt. It didn't end with her shithead friend, by the way. On Sunday we went out to buy vodka, and Edie picked up the guy who works at the liquor store.'

'What, she brought him home?'

'He had to finish his shift. I passed out so I'm not sure he actually did come.' She expected a reaction to her double entendre but got none. Oliver clearly wanted to change the subject.

They drank their coffees in silence.

'Well, Edie will be Edie,' Oliver said eventually.

'What does that mean?'

He looked at her over the edge of his cup. 'She'll always choose herself first.'

Beth thought about this. 'Doesn't everyone?'

Oliver shook his head. 'Not me. Not you.'

She liked that he included her in his circle of virtue, but the whole conversation had developed an edge she didn't quite understand.

179

Oliver stood up. 'Let's go do some work. Nice guys finish last, you know.' He stood back, polite as ever, as she went first. Behind his usual good cheer, she thought he seemed flat.

24

You couldn't exactly have called them drunks. They both drank after work, but then so did everyone else. It was impossible not to. The summer heat was such that all you needed was a frozen drink and your skin would waver and slide away in the most peculiarly pleasant way.

They sat at tables set out on sidewalks as the temperature nudged downwards a degree or two as a nod to evening, just enough so that any dampness of skin might catch any movement of air. There was childlike bliss in sipping soft grainy spools of frozen tequila and lime out of oversize margarita glasses till your eyes crossed and your brain began to spin. New

York City's specialist subject was Happy Hour: free baskets of tortilla chips instead of dinner, served with two-for-the-price-of-one helpings of sweet oblivion.

Beth noticed that Edie no longer bought alcohol from their local liquor store. 'It's too expensive,' she said.

Had Nick come up to the apartment that night?

Had the doorman called up and said, 'There's a gentleman here for you, his name is Nick'?

Had Edie said, 'Send him up', or, 'Would you ask him to come back another time? I'm feeling tired'?

Did he not show at all? Did she sit up in her sexy underwear till midnight, when it became screamingly obvious he wasn't going to show? Or did he show just at the last minute when she'd given up and dozed off? Did they have sex? Was it terrible drunken sex? Was it sex she couldn't remember? Was it sex that disgusted him because she passed out or threw up in the middle, or that disgusted her because he was clearly there for nothing but his own gratification? Was she avoiding him because he disappointed her or because she disappointed him? Or was he never there in the first place?

The instinct not to ask a difficult question is powerful. If Beth had been less sensitive to the unspoken desires of others, she might have just barged in and said, 'So come on, let's hear it. What *did* happen with cute Nick?' Did she not ask because she didn't want to know or because Edie didn't want to tell her?

Whatever had happened, the not knowing transformed gradually into a wedge big enough to jam open a door. Or jam it shut.

Meanwhile the flirtation with married Mike developed. Mike was good-looking and not short on charm. Beth could see the attraction, but she didn't like him. Edie claimed there was no possibility of heartache as she wasn't emotionally invested.

'I've invited him for dinner on Friday,' she said, and Beth's heart sank. Edie could do what she wanted, obviously. But was it her job, as best friend and non-paying guest, to aid and abet? That was less clear.

'Do you want me to go out?'

'No! I'll never forgive you if you do. Stand by me!'

Beth spoke carefully. 'Your married boyfriend's coming over for the evening. I'm seeing this as a one-outcome meal.' She paused. 'Am I wrong?'

Edie pouted. 'I wish you wouldn't be so blunt. I don't like to think about it in those terms.'

'Right, but …'

'OK, OK. Fine. But please don't go out. I might need you if things get out of control.'

'Out of control how?'

'Like if I decide after all I don't want to go through with it.'

'The sex?'

'Yes, the sex, the sex. Do we have to take the spontaneity out of everything by talking it into the ground?'

'No. I'm happy to pretend we have no idea what this evening is about. Why don't I pick up a deck of cards and some onion dip on my way home?'

'Don't be mean.' Edie sighed. 'What if I do want to have sex with him?'

Beth was silent. She had a hard time imagining Edie having sex with anyone. She had both the body and demeanour of a hungry child. Maybe that's what men liked.

But Edie was funny, smart and great company. She looked great in clothes. She looked great without clothes. Maybe she was fantastic in bed. Maybe men could tell she'd be fantastic in bed by her smile or the naked way she held your eyes.

The evening with Mike was possibly the most awkward Beth had ever endured.

From the first minute he and Edie arrived home, drunk, with their hands all over each other, she wanted to be permanently elsewhere.

'Beth, this is Mike,' Edie giggled drunkenly.

'You've seen him around. But don't say you've heard so much about him because then he'll think we talk about him when he's not here.'

'Hi, Beth.'

Beth smiled at Mike, but he didn't meet her eyes. Maybe he could see into her brain, where she was thinking, *Pregnant wife*. She'd been told before that her thoughts appeared on her face.

Mike clearly wanted to get on with the critical part of the date, but Edie insisted Beth stay while they ordered food and ate it.

He kept casting glances at the clock.

They made polite conversation about what it was like to be an intern, with Edie doing nearly all the talking. Mike looked as if there wasn't a subject on earth that interested him. At the first possible opening, Beth made an excuse and left.

'I'm really sorry, but I'm meeting someone for a drink,' she said, looking at her watch. 'It's been great seeing you again, Mike.'

Edie glared, knowing Beth's date was a lie. But she had to get out of the apartment.

After wandering up and down Broadway for half an hour, she found a phone booth and dialled Tom's number. It rang for ages before he answered.

'Yeah?'

'Hi Tom. It's Beth.'

'You again.'

'You busy?'

'No. What's up?'

'Not a lot.' She hadn't thought this far ahead. 'You guys missing me?'

'Why? You miss us?'

The reality of Tom. So much more irritating than the fantasy. 'My roommate's driving me crazy.'

'Join the club,' he said.

Well, that figured. 'So … you haven't rented out my room?'

'You wanna move back in? I wouldn't advise it.'

'I'm not that desperate yet.'

'Is it money? You can have it back.'

'That's OK. I didn't exactly give you notice.' *And I'm not paying rent here*, Beth thought.

A long pause.

'Look. I might need to come by sometime and get a few things.'

'Like what?'

'Just some things.'

'Sure. But there's nothing left in your room. I should know, that's where I sleep now.'

Interesting. 'Trouble in paradise?'

'Don't know what you mean. Dawn and I are happily settled in the ninth circle of paradise. Come on down and see for yourself. You'd be a sight for sore eyes.'

She felt reluctant to hang up. 'OK. I'll let you know when.'

'Anytime.' He hung up.

She walked home, let herself in silently. Mike's bag was still in the hall. She hurried to her bedroom.

It was after midnight that she heard whispering outside her room, and the apartment door closing.

She pretended to be asleep despite knowing that Edie would want to talk to her.

'Beth,' Edie whispered at her door. 'You awake, Beth?' When she didn't answer, Edie padded off back to her room.

Beth couldn't fall asleep for a long time.

25

Next morning, Beth found Edie in the kitchen with a box of pancake mix.

'I'm making pancakes of tragedy,' she announced, and poured Beth a cup of coffee.

'Huh,' Beth said. 'Are they made with tragic ingredients? Tears? Remorse? Do they taste tragic?'

Edie frowned. 'We'll see,' she said, stacking eight pancakes, pouring maple syrup over the top and comparing her creation to the picture on the box. 'Not bad,' she murmured, dug her fork in and lifted it to her mouth. 'Well,' she said. 'They taste of pancake and nothing but pancake. Need more maple syrup though.' She reached for the bottle and tipped more syrup over her tower.

'So, what makes them tragic?'

Edie sighed. 'They're infused with a deep sense of ontological futility.'

Beth sipped her coffee. 'Oh, for God's sake. Tell me everything.'

It made Beth feel slightly better that Edie said she would have preferred to spend the evening with her. The sex with Mike was OK, she said, but he didn't make much of an effort, just shut his eyes and went for it. 'I mean it was fine and all, but also kind of insulting. Bang bang bang. You know?'

Not really.

Edie said he'd been in such a hurry to do the deed, get dressed and get home that she ended up feeling dirty and depressed like she'd performed some sort of unpleasant service.

'Why didn't you warn me!' she cried, and Beth nearly burst out laughing. Edie smiled then. 'Well, why didn't you warn me harder? I can't help being pathetic.'

Beth snorted. 'Of course you can. Anyone can help being pathetic.'

'Not me,' Edie said. 'I'm a congenital ruin.'

'What does that even mean? You're the opposite of a ruin. And anyway, no one *makes* you a ruin.'

'My mother makes me,' muttered Edie, but her tone was apologetic.

'Don't be a victim. It's not attractive. Especially when you have a will like yours. You're stupid stubborn.'

'That's what my shrink says. Strongest victim he's ever met.'

'You sound like you're proud of that. It's horrible. You'd be the first to tell me to stop if I said something like that.'

'I'm not proud of it, just resigned.' Edie stuffed more pancake in her mouth. 'These are great. You want me to make you some?'

'Sure.'

Edie made another stack for Beth, though she only wanted two. 'It has to look like the picture on the box,' she said. When it looked sufficiently like the picture on the box, Edie passed over the plate. 'He wants to see me again.'

'Surprise, surprise.' Beth didn't like how cynical she sounded. 'Why wouldn't he? You're amazing.'

Edie's eyes filled with tears. 'Do you really think I'm amazing? I feel anything but.'

'Oh for heaven's sake, Edie, you're totally amazing. And you don't need to go out with Mike. You could choose anyone you want, preferably—'

'Fine, fine. You don't need to say it. But the thing is, I like him.'

'OK.' Beth stopped. Exhaled. Thought, *It's your life. And anyway, what do I know about sex?* 'Well,' she said, 'then go for it.'

'Exactly.' Edie smiled and looked at her friend.

'I'm having a shower and then going out food shopping. You wanna come?'

'Sure,' Beth said.

Beth got her bag and rejoined Edie, who was searching through the pile of shoes by the door for two sandals that matched. 'I wish we were lesbians,' she said.

'You do not.'

'I do. I want a best friend who'll also be my boyfriend. And really, men aren't that easy to like, don't you find?'

Beth wasn't sure what she found. Were men harder to like than women? It seemed impossible to generalise.

'Well, your mother would like that. Lesbian freeloader.'

'Even better.'

Edie buckled her sandals and slipped her arm through Beth's. They crammed awkwardly through the doorway together, Beth equal parts exasperated and amused. She pushed Edie sideways, and then they were hitting each other and laughing till they fell over in the elevator.

'You love me, you know you do,' Edie said. 'Say you love me.'

'I'm saving that for marriage,' Beth said.

'That and everything else.' Edie grinned back at her like it was a joke.

Beth frowned.

'Oh, come on,' Edie said, shoving her. 'Don't take everything so seriously.'

She knew what would happen now. Edie would hang off her arm, seduce her with compliments and kisses and jokes, and she'd feel churlish about being angry. Maybe she was too sensitive to brush off Edie's flashes of cheerful aggression. It probably meant nothing, but they annoyed her.

They arrived at the Food Emporium. First stop, the cheese counter, where they chose a chunk of Parmesan and a triangle of Brie, moving on to salami, spaghetti, vegetables half buried in ice, and fruit and grain granola. They bought a container of olives and Italian breadsticks. Gigantic artichokes seemed like an insane indulgence, so they bought two.

When they got to the checkout, Edie whispered to Beth: 'Watch this. I can guess how much it'll all cost.'

'You can?'

Edie scanned the two baskets. 'Twenty-two dollars,' she said, and when it came time to pay, the total was $22.35.

'How'd you do that?' Beth was impressed.

'I'll tell if you promise not to reveal my method.'

'Swear on my life.'

'It's easy,' Edie said. 'Count how many items you're buying. Ten items, ten dollars. Some more expensive, some cheaper but it always works.'

'Always?'

'Yup.'

'My God, if this ever got out.'

Edie looked serious. 'I know. You promised though.'

The impossibility of staying angry at Edie struck Beth with force. She was like an adorable wild animal baby – a lion or a leopard – playful, big-eyed and fluffy. And if the claws occasionally came out, well, it was your own responsibility, your duty even, to beware.

26

Edie went straight home with the groceries, and Beth made a detour to the nearest bank. As usual on a Saturday afternoon, everyone needed money. She slid her card into the entry slot of the bank lobby, clicked open the door and joined the line for the cash machine, thinking about Tom, and wondering whether she'd bother to see him after all.

The mugger appeared on her left, held a large handgun to her temple and looked apologetic. 'Give me all your money or I'll blow your head off,' he said, in an oddly neutral tone of voice.

Her response surprised her. She felt calm rather than panicked, and the irony of the situation almost made her laugh. *I wonder how much money he thinks I have, standing* as I am *in line for the cash machine. How dumb can you get?* She'd imagined desperate, angry, volatile muggers full of angel dust, adrenalin and class resentment. But this?

She wasn't sure whether no one had noticed the gun, or whether New Yorkers were just so pathologically nonchalant that no one would give up their place in line simply because a violent crime was in progress.

Everyone shuffled forward. She and the mugger shuffled together. After what felt like an improbably long interval, it was her turn at the machine. 'My limit is fifty dollars,' she told him. 'Is that OK?'

'Sure,' he said. And then, 'Sorry about this.'

In classic Stockholm syndrome style, she found herself feeling sympathetic. 'It's fine,' she said, and handed him the money with a small but friendly smile. He grabbed it and fled.

On further thought, she doubted they'd remain in touch.

No one tried to tackle him. No one shouted 'Stop! Thief!' No one came up to ask if she was OK, despite there being at least six other people behind her waiting for money.

Not knowing what else to do, she headed out the door. Her limit really was fifty dollars, so she couldn't get more cash anyway.

On the sidewalk, a guy came up to her. 'Did you just get robbed?'

'Uh-huh,' she said.

'Are you OK?'

'I think so.' Though to be honest, she felt a little shaky.

'I wasn't sure what was happening. Go home and call the cops,' he said. 'Not that they'll do anything, but you may as well keep the crime stats honest.'

'Right,' she said. And then, 'Thanks.'

'You need me to walk you home?'

'No,' she said. 'I'm OK.'

She didn't tell the doorman she'd been held up at gunpoint. It seemed silly. Lots of people got mugged in New York, and the guy had probably chosen her because she looked suburban. Which made it almost her fault.

Edie was shocked. 'Wow,' she said. 'Are you OK? I've never been mugged in New York. I get flashed sometimes. It happened once when I was about ten and I'd never seen a penis before. I kept looking at it trying to figure out what it was. But criminals can probably tell I was born here and leave me alone. Were you scared?'

Beth explained that she hadn't really been scared at the time, but she'd felt queasy on the streets coming home, looking around all the time, waiting for someone else to pounce.

'Not such a bad thing,' Edie said. 'You gotta have your wits about you to live here. I bet it never happens to you again.'

It wasn't really the reply she'd hoped for. But she was used to Edie's overblown reactions to her own tragedies and minimal response to everyone else's. It was just the way she was. Another person might have called it selfish.

Eventually she called the police. The desk officer sounded bored. 'You should come down and look at some photos,' he said, and Beth didn't dare say she wasn't very good at faces. The gun – now that was a different thing altogether. Tiny hole in the end. Flat barrel. She could pick that out of a line-up.

'OK,' she said. 'Should I come now?'

'We're pretty busy at the moment, maybe in a few hours.'

She'd expected more sympathy for being nearly murdered and in the end decided not to go. Nothing much had happened after all. He'd seemed to really need the money, for drugs probably, and she didn't think she could identify his face. Nor could she remember what he was wearing, or anything much except their odd exchange. She didn't particularly want him to be arrested and spend years in jail. He could have hurt her but hadn't. And he'd said sorry.

For some reason, that helped.

Beth thought about calling her parents but decided it would only upset them. Instead she sent a postcard of the Brooklyn Bridge, saying she'd managed to buy it for just fifty bucks, which she thought was a pretty good price. After all their warnings, she knew they'd laugh.

27

'He thinks if he proves how much better he is than the rest of us, they'll offer him a job at the end of the summer.' Edie lit a cigarette, and Oliver waved the smoke away from his face. 'But he's the only one of us who already has a degree and we're all going to college next year so he could afford to be less selfish.'

'Besides, no one's even mentioned a job,' Beth said.

'Doesn't matter. In his head there's a job and he'll make sure he's the one who gets it.' Edie somehow managed to talk, smoke and eat cafeteria lasagne all at the same time.

Oliver considered. 'He's the first in his family to go to college. You can understand him wanting to get a foot in the door.'

Edie snorted. 'It's no excuse for being an asshole. I've had to work with him this week, and though I say *with him* what I mean is *without him*. He's secretive and sticks to that Matt Eisen guy like glue. Lots of people are tipping Matt for stardom so Dan never leaves his side. It makes me furious. I don't know how you two coped.'

It wasn't really Oliver's style to compete. Beth figured he'd never had to.

'He takes any halfway interesting job for himself. He's so competitive,' Edie said. 'And the way he sneaks around – I could strangle him.'

'We're all competitive,' Beth said.

'But the rest of us have the decency to be polite about it.' Edie had started on a large chocolate brownie. Beth was still eating her sandwich.

'Maybe politeness is a luxury.' Beth had often

thought this. 'Maybe if you're not born into all this –' in a wide gesture, she indicated the newspaper and New York City beyond – 'you can't afford to be reticent.'

Edie ignored her. 'Jeanne says she's spoken to him a couple of times already. He's an idiot if he thinks they're going to offer him a job if he pisses Jeanne off.'

They fell silent as Dan approached their table.

'Hey, Dan.' Beth moved over so there was room for him. 'Did you hear I got mugged?'

'No. Really? You OK?'

'Yeah, fine. He was kind of an idiot. Held me up at gunpoint while I waited for the cash machine. Like he couldn't figure out why I was there in the first place.'

'Gunpoint? Whoa. Did you tell the police?'

'She tried,' Edie said. 'But they put her on hold for five hours and then hung up.'

'Not exactly,' Beth said. 'They said they were busy

and could I come report it at a more convenient moment. I took it as a lack of concern.'

'Well, I'm glad you weren't shot, anyway.'

'Gosh, Dan. Thanks.'

The conversation lagged.

'So, what's it like working with Matt Eisen?' Oliver managed to make his interest sound sincere.

'Good,' Dan said, through a mouthful of sandwich. 'I'm helping him research a big cover story, all about crime syndicates and bent cops. It's top secret, can't talk about it.'

Edie rolled her eyes at Beth. She turned to Dan. 'Aren't we supposed to be working together?'

'Are we? There's plenty of work to go around.'

Edie got up and left the table.

Beth got up too. 'I'll see you guys,' she said.

Edie was fuming. 'I've had it with him. Now do you see what I mean? I was right from the start. From now on he and Oliver can have each other. I'm telling

Jeanne I'm only working with you.' And she threaded her arm through Beth's.

Oh, Beth thought. She liked working with Oliver, was studying his easy manners, hoping they might rub off. In her family, nothing was ever simple. For as long as she could remember, her parents had seemed complicated and tragic, their secrets just beyond reach.

Oliver just seemed clean.

28

Mike spent weekends with his wife, so on Saturdays Beth and Edie did laundry, shopping and sleeping. But on Sundays, after Edie returned from her grand-mother's, they sometimes went out – to the Bronx for discount designer clothes, or down to Orchard Street where women's dresses, men's suits, and the heavy dark coats of Orthodox Jews hung high on hooks outside shop after shop, swaying incongruously in the heat.

Beth was fifty dollars down from the mugging, so she bought almost nothing, but enjoyed the sensa-tion of shopping, enjoyed watching Edie (with her bottomless allowance) add clothes to her already bursting closet.

Beneath the criss-crossing fire escapes of Orchard Street's tenement blocks, signs advertised Shoes, Hosiery, Dresses, Bags, Coats, Uniforms, Woollens, Underwear, Fabrics, Ribbons, Buttons and Notions. Signs on shops marked with prominent Jewish stars read: Bekishe and Shtreimel, Kittel and Yarmulke. And everywhere, everywhere, everywhere: Bargains, Bargains, Bargains. SALE! HUGE DISCOUNTS! SPECIAL PRICES! LAST DAY OF MARKDOWN!

'Bekishe and shtreimel,' Edie crowed. 'Kishkes and strudel!'

On their first trip to Orchard Street, Edie took Beth to the Orthodox bra-man who began to tut as soon as you came through the door, then went muttering to the back, returning minutes later with the correct bra, not at all interested in the size you told him you wore, or whether you liked the look of the one he chose. Beth shimmied her way through boxes, stacked shelves and trays of lingerie to get to the tiny cramped changing room at the back of the shop and had to admit that the one he'd handed her felt better than any bra she'd ever worn. He wasn't quite Gandhi or Einstein, but his skill was impressive. She bought the bra mainly out of appreciation for his world class talent, though it was expensive. She tried to think of it as an investment.

Afterwards they walked around the corner and ate knishes from Yonah Schimmel because it was so authentic.

'What flavour'd you get?'

Beth took a while to swallow. 'Potato.'

'How is it?'

'Tastes like cement. Yours?'

'Kasha. One hundred per cent Negev sand.' Edie inhaled a knish crumb and began to choke.

Beth whacked her on the back. 'Do you need the Heimlich manoeuvre?'

'A German manoeuvre?' Edie gasped with

laughter. 'Better you should leave me here to die. You can use what's left of the knish as my headstone.'

They gave up on knishes, dumped the remains in the trash and walked crosstown to Vesuvio for fennel and black pepper Taralli, a brown paper bag of each.

'The great thing about Italians,' Edie said, 'is that the stuff they make actually tastes good. It's practically anti-Semitic as a concept.'

'That's ridiculous,' Beth said. 'What about Zabar's? Or Katz's? What about nearly every deli in New York?'

'Fine. But you can do a lot of cultural damage with a knish.'

'Give me half a pound of corned beef on rye over anything you can buy at Vesuvio. And a half sour pickle.'

'Who's the real Jew here anyway?' Edie snorted.

'I'm as Jewish as you are.'

'Suburban Jew. Doesn't count.'

Edie had to win at everything, including being a

Jew. Beth didn't voice her opinion that having four grandparents gassed to death might bump her up whatever Jew list was going. Of course, she'd never mentioned her grandparents to Edie. Partly out of an obscure sense of shame. Being the child of Holocaust survivors imparted a taint she couldn't quite explain.

They walked back up MacDougal, through the Village.

'How's your new bra?' Edie asked.

'I'm not wearing it, am I? It's probably just hanging out at the bottom of the bag pining for a bosom.'

'A bosom? One single bosom?'

Beth considered the single bosom. '"Bosom" is such an awful word.'

'Whatever you do, don't lose that bra. It is a life-changing bra.'

'How am I going to lose a bra? Leave it accidentally in a phone booth?'

'Besides,' Edie continued, 'according to the bra

guru, it won't fit anyone else on earth. It's like Cinderella's bra. If the prince found it discarded on the stairs, he'd have to go around trying it on every woman in the land.'

'Why would I discard it on the stairs?' Beth munched a Taralli. 'I'm not sure I like the idea of being quite so unique. I'd like to have something in common, shape-wise, with my fellow females.'

'You're too scared of standing out. That's your problem.'

'Oh, really? That's my problem?'

'Being different is the best. Uniquity.'

'Not even a word.'

'Whatever,' Edie said. 'It's still the best.'

'Have I never showed you my hermaphrodite genitalia? My plan,' Beth said, 'which I am willing to share with you at this time, is to creep along under the radar and then when no one's looking, rise like a Valkyrie and take over the world.'

Edie laughed. 'Excellent use of "Valkyrie".'

'Thank you.'

But then Edie stopped in the middle of the side-walk and stared at her. 'You think you're joking but you're serious. You're secretly aiming for world domination while pretending to be a funny, grey little unfashionable girl from the suburbs.'

Beth blinked at the description. She looked at Edie to see if she was just playing around but she wasn't. A funny, grey little unfashionable girl from the suburbs.

That's how her best friend saw her.

29

Edie had stopped knocking on Beth's door after Mike left, knowing her friend was unlikely to answer. But on this evening she arrived home early, alone, and went straight to Beth's room. Her eyes were red from crying and she looked terrible. Throwing herself down on the bed, she wept piteously.

'Oh Christ,' Beth said, unable to hold out. She leaned forward and put her arms around her friend.

'It's not like Mike is my dream man or anything,' Edie sobbed. 'You have to understand. Sex makes me feel better about myself. But if I had to choose,' she hiccuped through her tears, 'there's no contest. I'd always choose you. Always. Only … I don't want you to be upset every time I go off with someone.'

'For heaven's sake, you don't have to choose. And you certainly don't have to choose me.' Beth was repelled by her own impulse to manipulate.

'I want to.'

'No, you don't. I'm just jealous.' She was just jealous. 'And worried about you.' Was she? 'And I liked it better when it was just us.' She had. Were Edie and Mike finished? Please God. 'You'd better tell me what happened.'

Edie nestled against her, sniffed, wiped her eyes. 'I think I'm in love with him.'

Oh. 'Well, I guess that's not a total surprise.'

'It is for me. I never fall in love.'

Beth sighed. 'What happened tonight?'

'It was Mike! He told me he was in love with me. He's so tormented, and of course he can't leave his wife now. I feel so sorry for him.'

For him? 'How long has he been married?'

217

Edie flinched at the question, or was it just the word? 'I don't know. Five years?'

'And has he cheated on her before?'

Edie frowned, as if cheating were the last thing he was doing. 'I didn't ask. He says he's never felt like this before.'

'I'm sure he hasn't.'

'Don't be horrible. Anyway, he wanted to go home and think about what to do, so we didn't go out tonight.'

You mean, you didn't stay in tonight. 'It doesn't sound like he's in much of a position to do anything. As you said.'

Edie looked glum. 'I know. It's so unfair.'

They sat in silence for a time and then Edie leaped up and said, 'Let's forget about Mike and send out for pizza.'

So that's what they did. And the subject was closed.

Later, alone in bed, Beth thought about the whole

fantasy of Mr Right. The promise that when you found him – partner, other half, soulmate – he'd be far better, more valuable, than any friend. In the meantime, you had to live through not knowing, uncertainty ruining month after month, year after dreary year, leading to a sense of life incompletely lived until a resolution could be reached. No wonder people threw huge wedding parties. Not from love, from relief. *Finally. We can get on with everything else.*

Beth considered that the duties of Mr Right would be far easier split among a committee. In practice this happened, but not officially. No one ever said, 'I'd like you to meet my partners: my husband, my mentor, my best friend, my sister.' Instead, the real players lurked in the background, uncredited. There was no ceremony for when you found a lifelong friend. And no divorce for when it went wrong either.

30

After their great reckoning and declarations of love, Edie and Mike spent every spare evening together. Edie never knew in advance when Mike would be free, but she invariably dropped everything – dates with Beth, appointments with Dr Lieb, even work – to be with him. It was always the same. They'd come home and, after the minimum of polite conversation, slink off to bed.

Not having a lot of other friends in New York, and sick of eating dinner on her own, Beth called Tom.

'Yeah, fine,' he said when she asked if she could come down.

He let her in and beckoned to the fire escape where he'd been smoking a joint. The utter squalor of the apartment was even worse than she remembered. How had she lived here? Crumbling and sordid, no right angles, not a single clean surface.

Sweating and uncomfortable from the climb, she crawled out behind him, took a drag when he offered the joint and held the smoke in her lungs till she started to cough.

'Easy,' he warned.

Within five or six minutes she felt fantastically stoned; swirly and vague and somewhere far away in her head. They sat together in happy silence while time passed and then Tom leaned over and kissed her and she kissed him back, not caring very much (she told herself) who he was. They kissed for what felt like ages, and then Tom reached behind her for a bottle of beer.

'Here,' he said, offering it to her. 'No glasses. Didn't expect company.'

Beth leaned against the side of the metal staircase and drank beer out of the bottle. Tom lit the joint again, but she'd had enough. One more drag and she'd slip gently off the metal platform and glide across the river to Hoboken. He inhaled. The paper burned with a soft hiss.

'Nice,' he said. And kissed her again.

Had he been thinking about her? Did it matter? He tasted pleasantly of grass and beer and kissing him felt nice. Sweet.

'Thomas,' she said.

'Mmm.'

'What would Dawn think?'

'Don't care.'

I don't either, Beth realised, surprising even herself. It was fine here, with no urgency, and no inevitable progression to bed, which could have been awkward because much as she didn't care about Dawn, she didn't particularly want her to walk in on them having sex. Even stoned there was no upside to that. And besides, did she even want to have sex with Tom? She wasn't sure. But to be away from Edie, with someone Edie barely knew, someone who cared about her in his own entirely peculiar but moderately sincere way, felt like a victory.

'I got mugged,' she told him.

'When?'

'A couple of weeks ago,' she said. 'At gunpoint. At a cash machine. The guy apologised though, in the middle of the hold-up. He didn't seem so bad.'

'For a crazy man with a gun.'

'Exactly. For a crazy man with a gun he seemed nice.'

Tom said nothing for a moment. 'That's a very strange story. You're an unusual girl.'

I'm unusual?

'Still, most people get mugged eventually.' Tom lit another joint.

'Don't worry,' Beth said. 'I wasn't hurt. Thanks for asking.'

He inhaled. 'A lot of people get shot or stabbed. Maimed. Killed. For no reason.'

'Thanks for that. I'd just started thinking I might get over it someday.'

'Best to be realistic.'

'He said give me all your money or I'll blow your head off.'

'No wonder you liked him so much.'

They didn't speak for a while, just sat leaning into each other.

Eventually she pulled free. 'I should go.'

He didn't open his eyes.

But when she tried to stand up, he took hold of her wrist and pulled her back down. 'Stay,' he said, and she was so touched by the request that she did.

He barely seemed to notice half an hour later when she got up, climbed back through the window and left.

Beth walked home. It took about an hour and a

224

half but passed without time; she felt like a pinkish cloud drifting slowly north.

Once in bed, she floated off to sleep, thinking thoughts she wouldn't remember in the morning.

She didn't get a chance to tell Edie about getting stoned on a balcony with Tom because the next day all Edie wanted to talk about was Mike. Which wasn't surprising. Beth's relationship with Tom wasn't nearly as interesting as Edie's relationship with Mike. For one thing, Edie would say it wasn't a relationship at all, and she'd have a point. What Beth felt for Tom was impossible to define.

When she and Edie did spend time together now, Edie talked incessantly about how smart Mike was, how he said he wished he'd met her before his wife, how he'd never wanted a baby but she'd stopped taking the pill without telling him.

'It sounds like it's getting heavy between you.'

'In a way,' Edie said. 'I mean, I do love him. But I figure it's his problem he's married and his wife is pregnant, not mine. If he's missing something from the relationship and I happen to come along, you can't exactly blame me.'

Interesting take, Beth thought.

'And the thing is, I feel so much better having a boy-friend than not having one, plus I really don't do well without sex. Dr Lieb says it's part of my neurotic com-plex and something I need to deal with. But I figure the best way to deal with it is by having lots of sex.'

'I thought you said the sex wasn't very good.'

'Well, it wasn't at first. But I think that's because he sensed he really liked me so there was a lot at stake. It's completely different now. Amazing in fact. We just click. You'll know what I mean someday.'

Oh, go to hell, Beth thought, and while Edie went on about how amazing Mike was, she drifted off in her head and thought about the fire escape.

The problem for Beth was that nobody really wanted her at either apartment. When Mike was at Edie's,

Beth's presence made everyone uncomfortable, even though Edie swore it didn't. In the Village, Beth was the understudy in Dawn and Tom's disaster of a relationship.

Tom didn't call her. So to get out of the apartment she walked the streets, looking over her shoulder for muggers who never appeared. She grew to like wandering for miles on hot summer nights, the air sultry and humid, the atmosphere like something out of a foreign film. Residential blocks were so quiet she could hear her own footsteps and she sometimes felt spooked by drug dealers hovering in the shadows. But if she walked down the avenues she always felt safe. Taxis sped past. Greengrocers were busy with people on their way home from working late. Occasionally she'd reach casually into the banks of shaved ice (heaped up for watermelons and papayas) and pull out a handful to cool her face and neck. People sat outside on stoops, ate in front of open windows, or perched on tiny balconies smoking and talking to neighbours. At about nine, the dog walkers emerged. Sometimes she started conversations by admiring their dogs. They always seemed happy to talk.

Beth peered into bars and restaurants where 'table for one' was more a statement of independence than an indictment. She drifted down to H&H where clubbers and night owls waited for the next batch of bagels. Even on a night this hot, no one wanted a cold bagel.

On a side street about ten blocks from home, she discovered a dusty sliver of a jewellery store – each item piled up in the window tagged with a price, from two dollars to hundreds. Everything was second-hand, antique, or just old, and she liked to look carefully, pretending she could choose one thing to keep. A pair of green amethyst earrings caught her eye each time, and she fantasised about having them appear as a surprise on her birthday, set in a black velvet box. She was sure there were real-life men who would notice what you liked and buy it to surprise you, though she'd never met one.

But why not buy the earrings for herself? Why not have a job that paid enough so she could afford the things she really wanted? Were the hypothetical earrings worth more, did they look and feel better, make her more glamorous, more excited by life – if someone else bought them for her?

Yes/No.

And what if the fantasy went wrong? What if she admired the green earrings week after week, but one week said, 'Ha ha, these are great,' and, just to make a joke, picked out a pair of gigantic paste diamonds she wouldn't be caught dead wearing in a snowstorm? And then what if he (the hypothetical he) got it wrong and bought *them* instead? What would she say? How would she turn the gift away without being cruel, without saying, 'You have no idea what I like, how could you possibly think I'd wear those awful things except as a joke? How could you think I'd want them (or, by association, you)?'

Occasionally, she wondered if it might be she who was wrong. She who, by virtue of her wrongness, would never inspire the right sort of love.

31

Oliver, Edie and Beth sat in Jeanne's office, waiting.

Jeanne hung up the phone with a dangerous expression. 'So, he's working for Matt Eisen now.' She shook her head and picked up the phone again. 'Matt Eisen, please.'

Everyone waited.

'Matt, it's Jeanne Pearce on the second floor. Is my intern with you?'

A pause.

'Well, could you send him down, please?' She hung up again, face stony, and stared straight ahead until Dan came in.

'Sorry, Jeanne. I've been doing stuff for the magazine this week.'

Edie looked at Beth. Dan couldn't resist bragging even to Jeanne. It was a bad move; any idiot could tell.

Jeanne's voice was icy. 'You work for me, Dan, not Matt Eisen.'

'I know, only I thought it would be OK if—'

'We'll continue this conversation after the meeting. I'd like to move on if you don't mind.'

The chill in the room was unmistakeable but Dan was defiant. Beth could see what was going through his mind. *I'm not going to back down on this story, it's my chance to do some real journalism and get a share of the byline, which Matt has hinted is a possibility. And he really likes working with me, he said so.*

She could also see what was going through Jeanne's mind. It was shorter and went something like: *I wish I'd never hired him.*

The contrast between Dan's utter determination and Jeanne's power to thwart him was a spectacle Beth preferred not to witness. Interns were expected to work hard, be grateful, follow the rules and not overstep the mark. Oliver was a natural because he knew he'd succeed just by existing. She and Edie were people pleasers, keen to follow the rules. For an instant she felt a twinge of sympathy for Dan.

With just three weeks left of summer, Jeanne handed the interns an evaluation form. Their comments would be used to adjust the programme next summer. 'Be honest,' she said with half a smile. 'It's too late for me to fire you now.'

'Thanks,' they said and got up to leave.

'Dan,' Jeanne said. 'Stay, please.'

Dan looked at his watch. 'Actually, I'm kind of pressed for time—'

'Sit.' Jeanne's voice was ice.

Oliver, Edie and Beth filed out. No one looked at Dan.

Edie grabbed Beth's arm. 'Come on. While Dan's getting flayed, we've got nine thousand files to return to the library. Then let's get lunch.'

Beth looked at her watch. 'It's only eleven thirty.'

'We'll be hungry by the time we've taken all this stuff back where it belongs.' She'd already grabbed a stack of files and was heading to the stairs.

Beth followed, thinking about the evaluation. *How I Spent My Summer Vacation*, she thought. *Hold the front page.*

32

Tom called a few days after Beth had stopped hoping he would. 'Come down to the Village,' he said.

'The Village? To do what?'

'See me, stupid woman.'

'What a nice invitation.'

'So?'

What would be the point of going to see him?

'OK. After work. Around seven?'

'Good,' he said, and hung up.

He'd made an effort of sorts; dragged a blanket out to the fire escape to make the metal grille more comfortable. And he didn't seem stoned when she arrived. She ate pretzels while he rolled joints.

The temperature had slumped into the mid-nineties and you could feel what might have been a breeze off the river, reduced to a mere sigh by the time it reached their block. The usual cacophony on the street gathered force as the sky turned orange a few miles away over New Jersey.

They shared a joint and made a start on the cold six-pack she'd brought. Beth ended up sitting with her knees bent up to fit in the small space, bare feet on the blanket, head tilted back, staring at the metal lattice of fire escape overhead. He leaned his back against her legs, handed her the joint over one shoulder and took a foot in each hand.

The warm resin swirled in her lungs and she wondered why nothing had ever felt as erotically charged as Tom's hands holding her bare feet. When he eventually turned to kiss her, she felt electric. But he was languid, dreamy.

What sort of thing was this, she wondered.

For the longest time they just kissed. The heat

softened the edges of everything, made all forays into sex abstract.

After a while they sat back, breathing softly and listening to the noise below. People blew horns, laughed, shouted, sang. Trucks revved their engines. Ambulances and police sirens shrieked a constant chorus. All you had to do was close your eyes and let the noise carry you off.

They didn't speak.

'Hey, Tom,' she said at last.

'Mmm?'

'Why is this the worst summer of your life?'

'Do we have to talk about this?'

'Can't you just tell me?'

'Figure it out.' He shook his head. 'I shouldn't be with Dawn. I shouldn't be in New York. I shouldn't be doing any of this …' He indicated the wider neighbourhood. 'This …'

She said nothing but wondered what he meant by 'this'. Working in a deli? Kissing her?

'What should you have done?'

'Applied for a master's, got a job in a lab. I'm making sandwiches. Because Dawn thought it would be fun.'

Beth considered this. 'It's just one summer.'

'You asked me a question.'

She wanted him to say that meeting her had made it worthwhile.

'Anything else you need to know?'

'No, I'm done.' She sighed.

'Good,' he said. And they kissed some more until it was late, and if he hadn't been living with his alleged girlfriend they would have gone to bed, but as it was, Beth had to go home, so she did. Reluctantly though. Because, despite the fact that he infuriated her, she didn't want to go.

33

No one really wants to hire an intern with a social life. The ideal intern has no life at all, nothing to do but be more attentive and hard-working than anyone in real life has a right to.

'You really should go home, Beth,' Jeanne would say. 'I'm paid to work this late, you're not.' But she didn't mean it. What she meant was, *If a person of my seniority, talent and experience is still in the office at 10 p.m., why shouldn't you be?*

As her social life with Edie waned, Beth fulfilled this expectation. Even when things were quiet she stayed late, ran the occasional errand and typed letters to school friends, retelling her life in amusing anecdotes that made better reading than living.

Mike seemed to be around the apartment constantly now, even on weekends. But occasionally he had to work, or his wife wanted him home, and that's how Beth and Edie spent their last ever day together.

'I'm going to see Clara,' Edie said. 'Please come, she really liked you.'

She thought I was good for you, Beth thought. And relented.

They took the express to Fourteenth Street on the first cloudy Sunday of summer. As they emerged from the subway, stuttering thunder resolved into a series of apocalyptic crashes and a downpour intense as a waterfall. They ran and shrieked in the glorious cool, glad not to have umbrellas, stamping in puddles like demented children. By the time they reached West Street, they were soaked through and laughing, and Beth felt nostalgia for the friendship that, for a while, had always felt like this.

240

In the elevator they shook themselves like dogs, and when Clara opened her door, she tutted and brought out towels.

'Do not drip on my floors, please.'

The girls dried themselves and Clara took down three small liqueur glasses, filling each with something purplish from a bottle with no label.

'It's plum brandy,' she said. 'Good for what ails you.'

Edie downed hers in one. 'Delicious,' she said.

Beth sipped hers.

'How are you both?' Clara asked. 'Tell me.'

'We're fine, Grandma, aren't we, Beth?'

Beth took this as a signal that there would be no talk of illicit affairs. 'We are,' she said. 'Working like dogs to prove we're worthy.'

'That's good,' Clara said. 'Now is the time to work, when you're young and hungry. By the time you're my age, a leisurely breakfast, an hour with a book and it's time for your evening cocktail.'

Beth thought Clara looked less well than before. She moved stiffly, as if her joints needed oiling. 'How are you, Clara?'

'As well as can be expected for a woman of my age.' She glanced at Edie, who sulked. 'Thank you for asking.'

They talked for an hour. Clara brought out portraits of the boys upstairs taken after their last visit, faces in saturated Kodachrome so vivid it looked as if they might speak.

'Vincent,' she said, pointing, 'and Stephane. So handsome.' Vincent and Stephane posed in tailored grey suits accessorised with traditional striped Cameroonian hats. On Vincent's lap was a Cameroonian death puppet, carved in wood and dressed in torn clothing. The two men looked beautiful as gods.

'I have your picture too,' Clara said, and brought out a single twelve-by-twelve-inch print of the girls in profile looking in opposite directions. She had caught the essence of each: Beth's uneasy scepticism and

Edie's defiance, against the rich mustard silk of the couch and her jewel-coloured embroidered pillows.

Something about the colours made it look more like a painting than a photograph. Edie just glanced at it ('I hate pictures of myself') but Beth was mesmerised. She'd never imagined she might feature in such a curious assemblage and it shifted the way she saw herself. Edie, of course, had a face designed to be photographed, but for an instant Beth could see the extent of her own beauty – the pure optimism of youth. Then it was gone.

'I've had one printed for you,' Clara said, and handed her a brown envelope, 'and one for you, Edie. Though I know you'll lose it.' Edie took the envelope with ill grace and Clara sighed.

They talked until it was time to leave. Edie slipped off to the bathroom and her grandma collected the little glasses.

Beth looked up and found herself caught in the beam of Clara's pale, sharp eyes.

'I know Edie is not an easy friend for you,' she said. 'But that's her fault, not yours. This is not an easy family.' And she carried the liqueur glasses into the kitchen.

Beth stared after her. Not an easy friend? You could say that again. It seemed a strange pronouncement from Edie's favourite person in the world, but she felt a rush of relief that someone else had noticed.

34

It was time to move back to the Village. When Beth called to ask if it might be possible, Dawn was typically laconic.

'You might as well. We're moving back to Philly on Friday anyway.'

Tom hadn't mentioned anything. Of course. Now she had to break the news to Edie.

She didn't expect it to spark a crisis. Edie was wrapped in a cocoon of self-interest. The space between them, once scarcely wide enough to slip a knife, was now a crevasse. She might make a fuss, protest that Beth couldn't abandon her, but in reality it would leave her free to have sex on the living-room floor with Mike. If that's what they wanted.

After work on Tuesday, she went to Christopher Street to say goodbye to Tom.

She buzzed, and when no one answered, pushed the broken door open and walked up to the fifth floor. The apartment door was ajar.

'Hey,' she called. 'Tom?'

The fans were off and it was stifling inside. She closed the door behind her. Tom sat on the sofa in the windowless living room in a haze of cigarette smoke.

'Jesus, Tom, aren't you hot?'

He looked stoned, and gloomier than she'd ever seen him. No smile, not even the usual ironic one. He shrugged.

Beth dragged the fan in from the bedroom and turned it on, pointing it to blow hot air out through the window in Dawn's room.

'What's up with you?' She opened the fridge,

found two cold beers and gave one to him. 'You look depressed. For a change.'

When he didn't answer she opened his beer and then her own. 'Come on. Let's go sit outside. You want to talk about it?'

'No,' he said.

Business as usual. 'I'm thinking I'll move back in here when you guys go.'

Tom nodded. 'Dawn said.'

'Might be a bit too weird to move back while you're still here. Especially as you're living in my room now.'

Tom was silent.

'It'll get better,' she said. Thinking, *Then worse, then better again.*

He looked at her. 'Yeah.'

'You don't think it's possible you smoke too much dope? They say it can make you depressed.'

'Who's they?'

'You know … medical experts.'

'Fuck them.'

OK.

They crawled out the window on to the fire escape and sat close together drinking beer. Eventually he put one hand on her knee, but nothing else. Maybe all along she'd blown up a casual flirtation into something bigger. Well, that was OK. It was incredible how a bit of human contact could make a difference. To her, if not to him.

They shared another joint and Beth heard a key in the door. Dawn crashed in with an armful of empty boxes piled up from the local market. 'Tom?' She sounded annoyed, crossed the room and stuck her head out the window. 'Hi, Beth. What are you doing here?' Tom hadn't moved his hand but Dawn didn't seem to notice. Or care. 'Are you going to help pack or not?'

'Not,' said Tom.

'I'd better go.' Beth clambered back into the apartment. 'See you, Dawn,' she said. And then called,

'See you, Tom.' She doubted she would ever see either of them again.

As she let herself out, she heard Dawn shout after her. 'Are you fucking my boyfriend?'

Beth closed the door and walked down the stairs at a steady pace. Once out on the street, she broke into a run.

35

The birth of Mike's baby came as a complete surprise, though presumably not to those involved.

Beth was shocked, as Edie had not raised the subject of Mike's wife for some time, and she had imagined it would be many months till the baby arrived. It hadn't occurred to her that Mike's wife could have been four or five months pregnant at the start of the affair. Or, as it turned out, seven and a half.

Somehow, after weeks of knowing all the facts, the reality catapulted Edie off a cliff.

It was mid-morning at work when the call came. Mike had presumably added Edie to the list of close friends and relatives waiting for the wonderful news. The baby was a girl. Melanie Jade.

'How did he sound?' Beth was genuinely curious.

'That's the thing,' Edie said. 'He sounded really happy and proud. You'd think he would have hidden it just a little. I mean, suddenly it seems my feelings don't count for anything.'

Beth blinked.

At first, Edie seemed OK. She couldn't exactly collapse wailing and tearing her hair in front of everyone, and besides, the interns were busy. She didn't mention the subject of the baby at lunch, but Beth watched closely for signs of strain. When she proposed a sympathy drink after work, Edie reached into the top drawer of her desk and pulled out a bottle of vodka, which she sloshed cheerily at her friend.

'I think you mean *another* drink,' she said. '*Another* drink would be totally acceptiple.'

Beth had planned to break the news of her departure after work. She figured it would be perfect – they'd leave on time, have a quick drink and a chat, she'd tell Edie she was moving out and then Edie would see Dr Liebermann the following day to sweep up the mess.

Damn, she thought. She couldn't be the second piece of bad news in one day. Not that Edie's mental health was her responsibility, but wasn't it just normal human empathy not to kick a person who was already down? Even if the circumstances of her being down were neither unexpected nor of anyone's making but her own.

And there it was again, that edgy mishmash of resentment and guilt. She was starting to recognise it as the third presence in their friendship. *Why me?* she thought. *Why do I always have to look after her?*

But at the back of her mind an insistent small voice said, *You bought into something when you moved in with her. You let her take care of you when you were sick, let her find you fabulous clothes, show you around at work. You took and you took, and now you don't want to give anything back? Shame on you.*

It was what her mother would say. It's what she herself might say to another person in this situation.

And yet.

'Margaritas?' Edie suggested as they left work together. 'There's a new place just around the corner and they've got a three-for-the-price-of-one opening-week offer. Dream come true.'

Great, Beth thought. Frozen margaritas it was. Three each.

Maybe the drinks would be small. Or weak.

But they were neither. They were large. They were strong. And, for some reason that ceased to puzzle Beth after the first, they were blue.

Across the table in the shimmering evening heat, Edie poured out her heart and cried as she sucked blue alcohol up through a straw like a child with a bubblegum slushie. Her heart contained an immeasurable hoard of misery.

She began with, 'This is the worst day of my entire life,' and, 'Why has he betrayed me like this?' But even she realised how bad that sounded and changed direction to, 'This always happens to me,' and 'Nobody loves me like I want to be loved,' followed by, 'I will always be alone, always,' which segued inevitably into, 'You're the only person in the world I can count on,' and froze Beth's heart to match her icy lips.

The tequila helped Beth make soothing noises. The fact that she was planning to move out imminently helped, but it confirmed Edie's 'I will always be alone' narrative and increased Beth's guilt. Occasionally she tried to interject a bit of perspective, a touch of 'Surely you went into this with your eyes open', but such reminders were entirely unwelcome. Besides, even she had to admit it wasn't the moment for 'I told you so'.

Huge tears slipped from Edie's eyes, and it was only when the bartender arrived at their table with a fourth margarita for each, and said, 'The gentleman at the corner table thought you might need cheering up,' and pointed to a good-looking guy three tables down, that she brightened somewhat.

'I think I should go over and thank him, don't you?' Edie sniffed back tears and made a brave effort to smile. She stood up unsteadily, holding on to the backs of chairs as she went.

Beth watched her go. Her friend's eyes were rimmed with kohl which had gone full raccoon with the tears. Her hair was a mess. She looked ravishing.

It was fifteen minutes before they returned together. Edie introduced her new friend (Joe? John?), and the three made bumbling drunken conversation until Joe/John said, *Are you girls interested in some dinner? There's a place I know nearby with great food*, and Beth said, *Thanks, but I hope you don't mind if I don't join you, headache from all the tequila, room spinning*, etc. At which point Edie put on her most concerned voice and said, *If you don't feel well, you really should go home and rest*, and what with all the *Are-you-sure*s and the *Yes-you-kids-go-have-a-great-time*s, Beth finally managed to stumble away, head genuinely spinning, and Joe/John and Edie went off together to eat.

With no memory of getting home, Beth's hangover drill took over: water, aspirin, bed. There was no sign of Edie in the morning, and as she got ready for work, the silence was a gift. She was happy that Edie had managed to replace Mike in the sex department so fast, which couldn't be a bad thing. Mike was bound to have less time to cheat on his wife now he had a new baby.

Beth's plan was to pack her stuff and move out on Saturday morning. She felt less guilty thanks to Joe/John. And would raise the subject of moving back to the Village over lunch, when Edie would no doubt be glowing and desperate to talk about her new conquest.

But Edie didn't come to work. And she didn't call Jeanne. When Jeanne came to ask if Edie was ill, Beth felt little inclination to cover for her.

'I don't know,' she said. 'She didn't come home last night.'

Jeanne's lips pressed tight, but Beth felt nothing but relief. Maybe Edie would stay out all weekend, making the conversation about moving out one that took place ex post facto. It was cowardly, but she was willing to be a coward if it made life easier.

After work on Thursday, when there was still no sign and no phone call, Beth's anger began to shift. What if she'd been murdered? Why hadn't she called just to say she was OK? Beth didn't know the last name of the guy she'd gone off with. She didn't even know his first name. John. Or Joe.

Would she be going to her shrink? Had she cancelled?

Beth spent the evening pacing and packing, expecting Edie to walk through the door any second. By ten, nothing. Eleven. Twelve. Should she call Edie's mother? The police?

But Edie was an adult.

So why hadn't she called? Adults didn't let people worry themselves sick over you.

Anger rose along with her fear.

She'd better be dead, Beth thought.

36

Friday passed with no sign. No call; not to her or to Jeanne, who scowled for most of the day and left a series of messages for Edie's parents on the phone in the New York apartment, which, naturally, went unanswered. Dan made unfunny jokes at Edie's expense.

Beth almost enjoyed everyone else's annoyance. It mitigated her own.

By Saturday morning, she'd begun to swing helplessly between panic and rage. *I'm sure she's fine*, Beth told herself one minute, thinking of statistics she'd provided for various stories about the demise of law and order in New York City. Two hundred thousand heroin users. Cocaine on the rise. Police numbers down thirty-four per cent. Crime up forty per cent. Eighteen hundred murders a year. Muggings too common to count.

The chances of Edie having been abducted and murdered seemed low one minute, inevitable the next.

There was no way Beth could return to the Village with her roommate missing. Anxiety made her head hurt. Surely, she'd just fallen for this new guy and was having a great time. *It's not my problem*, Beth thought.

But what if Edie was in trouble?

She called the police at 3 a.m. on Sunday morning.

Having spent the previous hours sleepless and increasingly frightened, she told them that her friend had last been seen with a guy called Joe, or maybe John, that they'd met at a Tex-Mex bar in Midtown on Wednesday night, that Edie had gone off with him to dinner and not been heard from since. Beth offered a detailed description, but the police weren't interested.

'When there's no evidence of involuntary disappearance, there's not a lot we can do,' the desk sergeant said. 'I'll log your call, but chances are your friend is having too good a time to check in.' She sounded bored.

'But she wouldn't not show up for work. And it's been almost four days.'

'Three days, honey.' The woman sighed. 'I've seen it before,' she said, in a tone that suggested she'd seen a lot of it before.

Beth said nothing.

'This may sound like a stupid question, but did he look dangerous?'

Dangerous? 'No,' Beth said. 'He looked like an advertising guy. Or a lawyer. Suit. Nice manners. Clean-shaven.' But wasn't that what serial killers looked like? Her mind raised an image of Ted Bundy.

'If your friend doesn't show up by Monday, call again. In the meantime, try not to worry. My guess is she's not dead.'

Great.

At 6 a.m., sleepless and buzzing with panic, Beth found Edie's address book and looked up Dr Liebermann's number. She hesitated before calling – what could he do? And at this hour on a Sunday morning? But if Edie had shown up to her appointment on Thursday, Beth could stop worrying. If she'd missed her appointment, Beth would call Edie's parents. As much as she really did not want to phone Dr Liebermann, she wanted to phone the Gales even less.

She dialled his number and a disorientated-sounding man answered.

'I'm so very sorry to bother you, Dr Liebermann, but this is Beth, Edie Gale's roommate, and I haven't seen her since Wednesday and wanted to know if she showed up to her appointment on Thursday so I could maybe stop worrying.'

There was a long silence at the other end of the phone.

'Hello?' she said.

'I'm sorry,' Dr Liebermann said. 'But Edie terminated her therapy six weeks ago.' There was another pause. 'So I'm afraid I can't help you.'

Beth froze. Six weeks ago?

After a stuttering apology, and Dr Liebermann saying he hoped Edie would turn up safe and sound, Beth said goodbye.

Terminated her therapy? How could she have failed to mention that? And the fact that she continued to be out on those nights? Where and with whom?

She called Edie's parents. They arrived at the apartment two and a half hours later, a few minutes before Edie herself unlocked the door and walked in, wearing the clothes she'd worn to work on Wednesday. For a split second, before she took in the scene, she looked happy.

Her mother, who until that moment had been pleading on the phone with the police, explained with polite frigidity that her daughter had just appeared, thank you very much for your time, so sorry to bother you when you probably had much better things to do.

Edie had almost no time to scan the loose group of three – their strained expressions, their anger and fear – before the shouting began.

37

Beth received a great deal more than her fair share of blame.

'How could you let her go off with some man she didn't know?' And 'What the hell made you think calling my parents was a good idea?' There was also a good deal of 'Is this how you repay us for allowing you to stay in our home?' and 'I will never speak to you again as long as I fucking live'.

The last suited her fine. She wanted to get out of the Gale household before Edie's mother put two and two together and realised that the substantial sums she'd been sending to pay for her daughter's therapy had been redirected. To what? Beth didn't care.

In the midst of the maelstrom, she grabbed her bags, straightened the bedspread and with a final glance around the room, walked out of the apartment.

The doorman gave her a comedy frown when he saw her luggage. 'Good luck, kiddo!' he said as she shouldered one bag and dragged the other around the corner to hail a cab, so she didn't have to tip him. Money was tight.

She paid the cab on the corner of Christopher Street with a strong feeling of déjà vu. Had it been only ten weeks?

The lock on the front door was still broken. Stragglers from Saturday night passed on the sidewalk without seeing her. She struggled up the dingy staircase, burdened with baggage and defeat.

Tom and Dawn were gone, along with Dawn's improvements, making the contrast with the apartment she'd just left almost unbearable. Her Debbie Harry poster swung from a single tack on the bedroom wall. But as long as she wasn't responsible for anyone's sanity but her own, she didn't care where she lived.

She ran the conversation with Dr Liebermann through her head again and again. Edie had quit therapy. It was something she'd talked repeatedly about doing. But to pretend the break was in the future, not the past? What was she doing on Mondays and Thursdays? Yet more dates with Mike? But why had she lied?

No matter which way Beth turned the question, it made no sense. At last, she gave up. *To hell with Edie*, she thought. *I no longer care.*

A few minutes unpacking, after which she fell into a deep sleep. The heat in the city had eased somewhat, but the emotional stress of the past few days made her feel a thousand years old. Most of all, she missed air conditioning.

At about two in the afternoon, the front door buzzer dragged her out of a drugged stupor. Probably some down-and-out trying every apartment on the off-chance. She certainly wasn't expecting anyone. She pulled the pillow over her head but the buzz persisted. With a groan, she dragged herself out of bed.

'What?'

'It's me.' The intercom managed to make any voice unintelligible, but she pretty much knew this one.

Christ. She buzzed.

'Hey,' he said when he reached the top of the stairs.

She stared.

'Sorry to wake you.' Tom looked at her, then at his watch. 'Huh.'

'I haven't slept much. It's a long story.'

'Had breakfast yet?'

'No.'

'Me neither. Let's go out.'

She pulled on some clothes, splashed water on her face.

He looked around at the empty flat, more dirty and miserable than ever. 'I like what you've done with the place.'

'Ready,' she said, and headed out the door ahead of him.

They walked to The Acropolis, got a booth, and ordered fried eggs, bagels, bacon, sausage, hash browns, coffee and OJ. Beth was starving.

'Tom?'

'Mmm.'

'What are you doing here? I thought you were leaving town with Dawn?'

'I did,' he said.

'And yet, miraculously, like our saviour Jesus Christ, you still walk among us.'

He didn't answer.

'Tom, for heaven's sake talk to me.'

'I'm sick of talking. Let's just eat.'

Sick of talking? They never talked.

She accepted more coffee from the waiter with the

roving pot. And then more again. A couple of times when she looked up he was staring at her. A couple of times he wasn't. When they were done, he asked for the bill and paid it before she had a chance to insist on splitting it. As they left, he took her hand and steered her back to Christopher Street.

'Can we talk now?'

'Nope.'

'When?'

He stopped and looked at her. 'What is there to say?'

What is there to say? How about *What are you doing here?* Or *What was all that stuff on the balcony?* Or *Do you actually like me or was kissing me just some sort of displacement activity?* Or … There was, in fact, quite a bit to say from her point of view. But she knew how he would respond. *Of course I like you, what would I be doing here otherwise?* And if she wanted to know how much, or in what way exactly, he'd just look at her blankly and say something like *Just under a mile*. Or *A cup and a half*. And he'd be right: how do you quantify how much you like someone? Beth supposed she wanted him to say, *With all my heart till the end of time*. Though what she'd do if those words actually came from him, she had no idea. Laugh, probably.

They trudged up the stairs to the apartment. She unlocked the door and he led her into her bedroom. Latterly, his bedroom. Turned on the fan.

They sat together on her bed. He pulled a joint out of his pocket and lit it.

'Do you have to be stoned?'

He didn't answer, just inhaled deeply, passed her the joint, closed his eyes, exhaled and then kissed her, pulling her down on to the bed as he did. It was hot and they were both sweaty. It felt good to dispense with clothes and she felt less self-conscious than she thought she would. The grass helped her once again enter that strange twilight underwater slow-motion place, only this time there was no

Dawn. No rush. Her attraction to him was inexplicable but complete.

At first Beth wondered whether she should be having sex with a person who remained a complete cipher to her after two months and who carried who-knew-what fatal disease because you just never knew these days. But he reached over the side of the bed into the pocket of his jeans and pulled out a condom, and by the time the light faded in the room and it was evening she was no longer a virgin, though she hadn't mentioned it to him and he hadn't asked. The act itself wasn't particularly what she expected, neither painful nor ecstatic. What she mainly felt was relief.

She fell into a doze on top of the sheets, her head in the crook of his arm. Eventually she heard him say, 'Ow,' and he pulled his arm free, stretching it out straight. 'Ow, ow, ow,' he said, and when the pain subsided, he turned away from her and said he had to go, and she said, 'Go where?' and he just said,

'Home,' and she was still stoned and didn't care where he meant by home, and the next time she looked he was dressed. He raked through her hair with one hand, arranging it on the pillow in an uncharacteristically tender gesture, and left.

Edie didn't show up to work again on Monday. She didn't call either.

At about eleven, Jeanne came in and asked if Beth knew what was going on.

'We don't live together anymore,' Beth said.

Jeanne tapped her pencil on the partition wall. 'Do you think you could call around and find out whether she's coming in.' It was not a question.

Beth thought about this. 'No,' she said.

Jeanne sighed, and left.

Dan was listening through the partition wall. He stuck his head around the corner.

'I can't believe you said no, just like that,' he said. 'God, you've got balls.'

But Beth was shaken. A small part of her wanted

273

to call Edie and find out how she was, why she'd lied about Dr Liebermann, what went on with Joe/John, what had happened with her parents. The rest of her never wanted to see Edie again.

Dan lingered at the edge of the partition. 'Do you think she's gone for good?'

She looked at him. 'What do you mean? Dead?'

'Nah,' he said. 'I mean off the radar. Not finishing up here.'

'Why do you care?'

'Ha ha.' The joke was forced. 'Less competition for the rest of us.'

Something flared. 'Who are you competing with, Dan? The rest of us are going to college in a couple of weeks.'

He stared at her. 'Everything in life is a competition. The sooner you figure that out, the better you'll do.'

The better you'll do? She wanted to shout, 'I don't want to do better, not by your stupid rules.' His ethos infuriated her. Work harder than everyone else, screw your friends, make as much money as possible, win a Pulitzer, die famous, rich, friendless.

Some success.

Dan disappeared. Beth sat very still and tried to imagine a future for the four of them. The places they might live. The jobs they might do. Oliver was obvious. But she couldn't imagine any of it for her or for Edie. The future looked entirely opaque.

Dan's future, on the other hand, was not in doubt. A job that was never good enough, a wife who never made him happy. A nagging sense of inferiority to people like Oliver.

If she'd liked him more, she might have pitied him.

38

Edie didn't come back to work.

Beth accepted that she would probably never get the real story. She told herself she didn't care, and only vaguely hoped the answer didn't involve forced incarceration in the rich person's version of a mental hospital or a dramatic suicide attempt, but her imagination stopped there. She figured it was more likely that Edie had been dragged back to East Hampton where her parents could keep an eye on her. Edie would be miserable, but Edie would be miserable regardless.

The three remaining interns had to pick up the slack. Three, that is, if you counted Dan, which you couldn't, because of Dan being Matt Eisen's personal flunkey. A combination of outrage and extra work sapped Beth's energy, and once her energy was gone, she switched over to adrenalin. Oliver was busy too, and they staggered their lunch hours to keep everyone covered.

One evening as she waited for the review of a new musical to be filed, she noticed Dan, hard at work, bent over his typewriter. She hesitated for a long moment. But they were the only two people on the floor.

'What are you doing here? Typing up notes for Matt?'

'Nah. Article's done. Just trying to clear my desk and finish a job application. If they don't keep me on, I can't afford my apartment. I can barely afford it now. And going back to Michigan.' He looked miserable. 'I just can't. I have to get a job, waiting tables. Anything.'

'But you went to Yale.'

'Lots of people went to Yale.' Dan sighed. 'I didn't get my byline.'

'That's too bad.' She felt a twinge of guilty pleasure. 'Could be worse. I've got four years of classes and essays ahead.'

'*A good education is never wasted.*'

Yeah, duh. 'Who said that?'

'My father. He never had one.'

Dan never let up on his deprivation narrative.

She wanted to say, *My father was put on a train by his parents at the age of seven and never saw them again. He had to start school in a language he didn't speak. And yet* he *managed to get to college.* But she didn't.

Instead she said, 'I kind of hate to leave all this just when I'm getting the hang of it.'

He looked at his half-filled application. 'You want to get a drink? I've had enough of this place for one day.' He sounded almost shy.

'OK,' she said. 'They can file without me tonight.' She ran to tell the theatre critic she was going.

'Have a drink for me,' he said, without looking up. 'I'll be here all night thinking up something nice to say about the musical calamity of the season.'

'Guess you can't say that?'

He glanced at her. 'No.'

'Good luck then.'

They went to a bar Dan knew in Hell's Kitchen with graffitied plywood walls and live music in the basement. The atmosphere between them was awkward, but that was nothing new.

'So, what happened with Edie?' Dan asked. 'I thought she liked her job.'

'No idea. She's not the world's most stable person. We haven't talked since last weekend.'

Dan frowned. 'I thought you were attached at the hip.'

The beers arrived.

'We were,' Beth said. 'But then she started sleeping with Mike and he was at our place all the time, only of course it's not our place, it's hers. Then his baby was born – and she went off with a guy she met in a bar, and I thought she'd been murdered. And I discovered by mistake that the two nights a week she said she was seeing her shrink was a lie. Blah blah blah. A mountain of half-truths. I'd had enough.'

Dan looked at her. 'Edie did my head in. I shouldn't say that. I know you're friends. Were friends. But the way she acts. It's …' There was something in his voice.

Beth frowned. 'What?'

'Nothing.'

'Nothing?'

'She came on to me once.'

'What?' Beth's eyes widened.

'Right at the beginning. I wasn't interested. And then she started hanging out with Mike. And then Oliver – you knew that, right?'

'They worked together.'

'Uh, not work.'

'*Not work?*'

He shrugged.

'Are you kidding?' Beth stared at him. 'But Oliver's gay.'

Dan looked puzzled. 'Where'd you get that idea?'

Beth's stomach dropped.

'I'm sorry,' Dan said, uncomfortable. 'I figured you—'

She shook her head, as if trying to shake thoughts from it. 'No, I'm sorry. It's fine. Only … are you sure?'

'Oliver doesn't exactly confide in me. But I'm pretty sure he's not gay.' He frowned. 'You know Oliver liked you, right?'

She stared.

'But you made it clear you weren't …'

Beth struggled to control her face. *Oh hell*, she thought. 'Edie warned me off you both. From the start. Told me …' In agitation, she stood up.

Dan half stood as well. 'We could talk about something else.'

Beth fell back on to her chair. She couldn't speak.

She'd never had reason to question Edie's line on Oliver and Dan. Oliver was too gay, Dan too ambitious. Her mind jumped back to the picnic in the park when she'd called him Ollie. Mondays and Thursdays. Where had she gone instead?

The world flipped. Oh, God.

Dan cleared his throat, shifted uncomfortably. 'I feel as if I'm missing something here. I'm sorry about Edie and … everyone.' He paused. 'There's not something between you and her—'

'No,' Beth said. 'Of course not.' He was such a jerk.

'I just wondered.'

'I have to go.' Any second she would burst into tears. She shoved back her chair and stood up once more.

As she stood, however, a fault line in her brain began to fracture. Tectonic plates slid free, heaving a vast wave of repressed energy to the surface. Hurled upside down and sideways by the surge, Beth began to laugh, inaudibly at first, and then more, and louder, until her entire body was possessed, shaking with hilarity. 'Oh!' she gulped. 'Oh, I'm sorry. I can't. I just …'

What a great journalist! Missing the gigantic looming story directly in front of her eyes. Tears of mirth poured down her face. She gasped for breath.

'You OK?' Dan asked nervously. 'You want me to get you a glass of water? Or a cab?'

Laughter rose up in her anew. A glass of water? 'I have to go,' she gasped. 'Sorry, Dan.' She held her sides. *Oh, God, what a fool.*

'I'll come as far as the subway with you.'

'No, no, it's fine,' she said, composing herself for an instant before the mirth surged through her again. 'Thanks for the beer.'

When she looked back, he was still staring after her, his face puzzled and forlorn. He waved. She couldn't help herself, turning away before her laughter erupted once more.

She wasn't laughing at him.

Despite the heat and the terrible apartment and all that had happened today, this week, this summer, Beth slept soundly and deeply and the next day woke refreshed. She rose early, walked to work, went straight to the bathroom, locked herself in a stall and sat with her head in her hands, thinking, *I've been mugged. So credulous, so blind. I should have recognised the signs, seen Edie for what she was.*

But she couldn't find the tragedy in it anymore and when she collected herself and emerged from the cubicle, she stared in the mirror and thought: You look better. Older. Lighter. She returned to work, humming.

Around mid-morning, Dan stuck his head in. 'You OK?'

'Just waiting on the editorial meeting.' Even Dan didn't annoy her today. 'They should have been out by now. Nothing to do but get wired.' She held up her coffee in a toast.

Dan was restless. 'I really need something stronger than coffee.'

Poor Dan. In mourning for his lost byline. 'Isn't it a bit early? Try Edie's top drawer.'

He did, pulled out the half-empty bottle of vodka, unscrewed the top and emptied it into his coffee.

'That can't taste good. I'll leave you to it,' she said, and gathered up a thick file of research requests.

When she passed Oliver in the hall, she hesitated for a moment and then smiled at him. A genuine, unselfconscious, ever-so-slightly rueful but nonetheless heartfelt smile.

He frowned slightly, hesitated.

She walked on.

39

Beth stayed alone in the Village apartment for just over a week. She worked late. Went in on Saturday. Avoided talking to people about Edie, which wasn't easy. Everyone wanted to know where she was. If she was OK. Each time, Beth said she was sorry but she didn't know.

Early on Sunday morning the buzzer rang. Beth was fast asleep in the sort of dead deep sleep it takes ages to throw off. But the noise persisted and with a groan she looked at her watch. Seven fifteen.

All she heard from the intercom was a distorted alien voice saying what might have been her name. She buzzed, shuffled to the door in her sleep shirt and peered out.

The footsteps on the stairs were familiar.

'So, Mr Bond,' she said. 'We meet again.'

Tom said nothing. He just looked at her, raised an eyebrow in the way of greeting and squeezed past into the flat. He had a paper bag in one hand.

'You look awful,' she said. 'Why does everyone look awful all of a sudden?'

'Thanks. You … huh.' He frowned. 'You look good.'

'Right.' She hadn't removed the eyeliner she wore to work so it was smudged under her eyes. Her hair was unspeakable. She wished she was wearing more clothes.

Neither of them spoke.

At last, she sighed. 'So, what are you doing here?'

'Seeing you.'

Same old Tom. 'All the way from Philadelphia?'

He nodded.

'Why, Tom?'

'I broke up with Dawn.'

'Well, congratulations. It's about time. You were the stupidest couple I ever met. No offence.'

'You haven't met enough couples.'

'Why'd you stay together so long anyway?'

He shrugged and led her into the other bedroom, opened the window and pulled her out with him on to the fire escape. Something about the way he led her around by the hand made her feel like a child.

'Here.' He pulled two cardboard cups of coffee from the paper bag.

It wasn't easy sitting on a fire escape in nothing but a T-shirt that only came to mid-thigh. She pulled up her knees and dragged it down over her shins.

They sipped coffee in silence.

'Tom. I'm obviously delighted to see you but what are you doing here practically in the middle of the night?'

'I wanted to see you,' he said.

Oh my God. 'Why?'

'I broke up with Dawn because of you.'

'Because of us fooling around?'

'Because I never felt anything with Dawn.'

'You were together three years. Maybe it just got old.'

'No.' He looked almost angry. 'I never felt anything real with Dawn. Ever.'

'OK,' she said, in a conciliatory tone. 'OK. Fine.'

'Listen,' he said. 'Please. Just for a minute.'

She listened.

'With you it was different. I wanted to say thank you.'

Thank you? 'For what?'

'For being *a person*.' He shook his head impatiently. 'Your feelings aren't …' He searched for the concept. Pressed both palms to his temples. 'Blank.'

Was that unusual? She wanted to laugh but didn't dare start. He was deadly serious.

'Because you're not being someone else or being cool or being anything. You think everyone's like you, but they're not. That's what I came to tell you.'

The conversation was too serious. And too strange. 'Does this mean you're madly in love with me?' she asked, in what she hoped was a light-hearted tone.

Tom rolled his eyes. 'Oh, love. That doesn't matter.'

'Why doesn't it matter? It matters to me.'

'So you love me?'

She liked him. She liked him in spite of the fact that he was difficult to like. She liked kissing him. She liked sex with him. But could you love someone you couldn't even have a conversation with? She did love him. In a way.

'It's important to me,' Tom said. 'Knowing someone like you exists.'

'Someone like me?' Beth frowned. 'Why not me?'

'You know why,' he said.

She had no idea why, though she liked the credit his answer gave her for emotional sophistication. But if he cared about her enough to come all this way, why didn't he want to go out with her, to at least have some kind of thing where they met every few weeks or months, or whatever? An actual relationship.

Thinking about it more, she wondered if maybe she was more a life preserver than a girlfriend, a ladder to help him to climb out of the unmoving sea of his relationship with Dawn. Another 'relationship' that wasn't what it seemed.

On the other hand, he'd come a long way to tell her that she was the real thing. Not real enough for him, obviously, but still.

She leaned forward and kissed him. It seemed sad that their relationship had no future. No past and barely any present either, to be honest. Why was it so disappointing when someone you didn't want to be with didn't want to be with you either?

They stayed like that on the fire escape as the street below stretched and yawned and slowly came to life with the night shift heading home from clubs and the day shift heading out for breakfast. Christopher

Street barely paused for Sunday morning. Then by invisible mutual agreement they went back to bed and had slow sweet sex, during which he avoided her eyes.

At about two in the afternoon, he got up, put his clothes on and went out, and she wondered if he was gone for good. She really had no idea what he might do.

But twenty minutes later he returned with beer and a box of doughnuts, which they ate in bed, leaving crumbs that she'd have to clear up before the roaches organised a charge. They had sex again and then again, and for a moment she did love him.

It was late when at last he disentangled himself, kissed her briefly and left. Where was he going at this hour? Did the trains to Philly even run this late? It felt final, but she admitted to herself that with him you just never knew.

When she thought about it, it had been an entire summer of not knowing. The minute the world came into focus, she'd turned out to be mistaken, looking at some parallax view.

What you see, she thought, *is not what you get. What you see is only what you see.*

But she could live with that.

40

With just a few days left of her internship, Beth felt a sense of excitement she couldn't pin down. She suspected it had to do with survival, the conclusion of all those firsts: first job, first time away from home, first New York friend, first sex, first hold-up at gunpoint (and preferably last), first betrayal. A series of successes and disasters in such quick succession it would take months, maybe years, to digest it all.

At work she knew her way around every corner of the building, knew where every blind door led and what was in every closet. She knew most of the staff by name, an accomplishment people who'd worked there years couldn't match. She knew how the systems worked and how to get around them. How to fast-track information and picture requests, use the microfiche library, who placed the house ads and how to get them resized in a panic if tomorrow's paper had a hole.

Some of this knowledge she'd picked up on her own, but most she owed to Edie, to Edie's insatiable curiosity and talent for networking, her passion for talking to everyone, knowing everything – from what was the big story of the day to what time the bagels arrived at the cafeteria.

You had to start somewhere. Edie's motto turned out to be perfect for diving in when you didn't know what you were doing, were worried you might make a mistake, were tempted to run away.

Thanks to Edie, Beth knew what pretty much everyone at the paper did, from compositors to reporters to copy-editors to advertising and sales promotion. Edie had taught her how to belong, how to make herself useful, how to think about the other person so her smile didn't look weird. She'd taught her to get over herself and concentrate on the job, which turned out to be one of the most important lessons she would ever learn.

Edie also made her avoid the other interns because one was gay and not interested in her and both were beyond the pale. Edie invited her to stay in her beautiful air-conditioned apartment and brought her Chinese food when she was sick and depressed and miserable. She didn't ask for anything in return except that Beth listen to her stories and believe her version of truth. Edie took her to Orchard Street and Yonah Schimmel and the Met. To the Empire Diner. To the book room. To the roof for lunch. To Leo's.

Beth went over the tally sheet in her head, trying to make it add up.

What had begun as treachery had morphed into something else. She had been through fire and was stronger for it. Forged in the flame of a New York summer.

And what have I learned? she asked herself.

That no one friend could give you everything.

That complex friends came with complex agendas.

That liars tell the best stories.

41

There was no formal farewell party for the interns.

There was no Edie, for one thing. And Oliver only came in for a few hours on the morning of their last day. Beth was reading the paper when he stuck his head in her cubicle to say goodbye.

Beth looked up. 'My God, Oliver, did you see this story?'

He came and peered over her shoulder. 'Another horrible murder.'

'Too horrible.' A heavily pregnant woman had been stabbed in the stomach and pushed off the roof of her ten-storey building in East Harlem. What she was doing up there, and who her assailant was, no one knew. But it màde Beth glad to be leaving New York. She had become accustomed to horrible murders, daily acts of blood-freezing atrocity that no longer froze her blood.

Oliver said goodbye and told her to keep in touch.

'I will,' she told him, thinking it unlikely.

At 5 p.m., Jeanne invited them to her office, where the drinks cart had been rolled in, and a handful of people from different departments congregated for a free glass of something. The event didn't match the momentousness of the summer in Beth's head. Glancing around at the people chatting and drinking, she was struck by how none of it held any particular significance for them. Interns came and interns went, and no one would think of this summer's group ever again.

It seemed odd how incredibly intense every encounter had felt, every personal and professional event etched on the surface of her brain. But only on her brain. Not theirs.

Edie was gone, Oliver had left and Dan looked visibly deflated. Even at the last he was trying to pin Matt Eisen down for a job, or at least a reference. It made Beth cringe. She'd heard enough about Matt Eisen to understand his agenda. He'd been nice to Dan as long as he was handy, but the carrot he dangled was not a metaphor for advancement; it was just a carrot.

When the alcohol ran out, people drifted back to their desks or left for home. Some called *good luck* as they went, more didn't. Beth wanted to hug them all, thank everyone – for everything.

A few people stayed to chat until Jeanne's phone rang and she turned to them saying she had a meeting. She thanked Beth and Dan for all their hard work, told them to stay in touch, shook hands with Dan, and was gone. Beth noticed Dan looking after her, understanding at last that there was no job.

And then it was just Dan and Beth with a few meagre belongings packed into cardboard boxes:

reference books, notebooks, pilfered pens, a couple of good luck cards. They left the department together, waved goodbye to the guy on evening reception, let the revolving doors revolve behind them. Beth secretly wished there'd been confetti, or fireworks; something significant to mark the occasion.

Dan said his sister was down from Michigan, so they parted quickly, both anxious to get away.

As she walked back to the Village, she thought of her parents. Her father leaving Germany with his sister, being separated and settled with a non-Jewish family in England. After the war, his aunt found them both through the Red Cross and brought them to New York. He'd been just nine when he came to America, speaking with an odd mix of German and English accents. His sister was just five. His parents didn't survive the war.

Her mother's family died in Poland. She and her older sister had been sent from Berlin to cousins in the Netherlands and then to Brooklyn, and when her mother started school, no one believed the stories she told of how things were for Jews in Europe. So she stopped telling them.

In every ending is a new beginning, Beth thought. All you have to do is survive.

All at once she felt a great rush of gratitude to New York. The city included everyone. The tired, the poor, the huddled masses, the interns, the screwed-up, the eccentric. The nymphomaniacs, the dangerously ambitious, the new and the old, the gay and the straight. The pregnant woman on the roof. And whoever pushed her off. The Kindertransport children. The refugees. The lost and the found. The still searching.

Beth turned uptown towards the light bouncing off a thousand skyscrapers. People always forgot to tell you how beautiful New York was, she thought. All those shafts of light. Blinding. Illuminating.

42

Within a week of arriving home to Providence, it was time to pack again. Beth spent the morning filling a large suitcase with everything she needed for college, realising it wouldn't close, throwing things away, repacking, and then starting all over again.

When the phone rang, she ran to answer. 'Hello?'

'Hello,' said a small voice.

'Edie?' Despite herself her heart leaped. Well, at least Edie was still alive. Now she could tell her to fuck off.

'Beth, I had to talk to you. My grandma's dead and the only person I can tell is you. I haven't stopped crying. I'm a total orphan now. Even my mother doesn't seem to care. Beth? Are you there? Are you still speaking to me? Please say you are.' Edie was sobbing. 'I don't blame you for not speaking to me, I didn't mean it. Any of it. I'm sorry. Really sorry.'

Edie's delivery irritated Beth, as did her not-so-subtle attempt to deflect blame and attract sympathy. She felt Edie was holding her grandmother's death in front of her like a shield. *You can't be angry at me*, she was saying, *I'm too sad!*

Beth kept her voice even. 'I'm sorry about Clara, Edie, but it doesn't change things.'

'I can't help how I am—'

'You *can* help it, Edie. You just *don't want to*.'

The voice turned small again, like a child's. 'I didn't want to share you with them. I wish I could take it back.'

'Too late,' Beth said, and hung up.

43

Beth didn't major in journalism. Calamity, catastrophe, disaster – the communal surge of triumph at every earthquake, every military coup, every pregnant woman stabbed and thrown off a roof. She couldn't face it. Even reading the news every day depressed her.

Tom came to see her at college, two weeks into her first term. No warning, of course, just a knock on the door, as if Philly and Chicago were three stops away on a local bus. In her tiny room, he sat on the only chair, looked around briefly and then pulled out a joint, inhaling deeply and passing it to her so things could be normal between them once more.

Same old Tom, she thought. But the grass made her giddy and stopped her caring. He was here. So was she. For whatever reason she still felt attracted to him.

They undressed in the usual languid haze. Sex with Tom reminded her how lonely her new life was; she felt grateful to him just for being familiar. She liked the smell and taste of him and how he became easier and more intimate when stoned.

'What's it like here?' he asked her.

'It's OK,' she said. 'I don't know many people. Big city, et cetera. How's Penn?'

'OK.' He didn't elaborate.

'Ever see Dawn?'

'Nope.'

'Do you miss her?'

'Nope.'

'Tom, what are you doing in Chicago?'

'My ex-roommate is getting his master's here.'

'So, you came up from Philly in the second week of term to see your ex-roommate?'

'I'm staying with him. I have an interview.'

'For … your master's?'

'Biochemistry.'

'Oh.' She didn't really know what biochemistry was.

She dozed off, waking at 3 a.m. to find him putting his clothes on.

'Are you going?' She felt looped in trippy dreams, unable to reach the surface.

'Go back to sleep, Beth,' he said. It was the first time he'd ever used her name.

The next day she felt empty and sad, and wondered if seeing him just made her feel lonelier. On balance she thought maybe it did. She wanted a boyfriend who would stay all night and go to breakfast with her in the morning. There never was a morning after with Tom.

He had brought the summer back to her, and with it a fleeting sense of calamity. Her brain wouldn't touch on Edie. Even a glancing thought tangled her in unmanageable emotions.

There was another knock at her door and for an instant she thought, *Here we go again.*

But it wasn't Tom. It was a guy from the floor above. She'd met him in freshman writing class, required for all first year students. He'd missed a class and needed notes.

'Tell me your name again?'

'Adam,' he said.

'Adam, OK,' she said. 'We have to write a *How I Spent My Summer Vacation* type of essay. I think it's supposed to be ironic. Impossible to tell with that teaching assistant. He said, "Make it fresh."'

The look of pure horror on Adam's face made her laugh.

'I spent my summer in a lab studying mutations in worms,' he said morosely. 'That's what I think about pretty much all the time.'

'Well, it'll make a change from all the essays on sex and death,' she said.

'My experiments are kind of about sex and death,' Adam said. At the look on her face he smiled. 'On a mitochondrial level.'

'Well, there you go. You're halfway there.'

As he was leaving, he asked if she was going down to lunch, and she said she was, and they were both relieved to have someone to eat with.

They sat with cafeteria trays between them and talked. He was funnier than he seemed at first. But in the middle of their conversation, she noticed that his eyes swam with tears.

She peered at him. 'Are you OK?'

And just like that, he began to tell her how he'd had sex with a much more experienced guy in his home town at the beginning of the summer, and how pretty much no one on earth knew he was gay, not his family or his friends from home, or anyone here, and how he was supposed to be getting the results of an AIDS test today at the student sexual health clinic. He raised his hands to hide his face.

Beth looked at him. How awful to be alone at a time like this. 'I'll go with you,' she said.

He shook his head. 'I don't even know you.'

'It's fine.' She realised it was. He seemed nice and it was the least she could do.

'What about your classes?'

She checked her watch. 'I don't have anything till three. That gives us plenty of time.'

'Are you sure? You're not worried about getting AIDS?'

'Not unless you're suggesting we have sex first.' Beth smiled at him. She thought about how worried he must be, how much he appreciated her small offer of kindness. And on impulse she added, 'I'm pretty sure the test will be fine.'

She had no idea if the test would be fine. If it was positive, he would probably die. But right now, it was easy to make him feel better.

You had to hope for the best, she thought.

You had to start somewhere.

Have you read

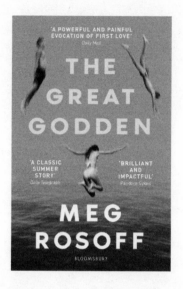

A timeless book that crystallises a moment of
growing up

'A sun-drenched coming-of-age story ... seductive
and elegant ... The heady nostalgia and sweet ache
of first love and lost innocence recall classics such
as *Bonjour Tristesse*' – *Observer*

AVAILABLE NOW!